What Are We Fighting For?

Brian Moses performs his poetry and percussion show in schools, libraries, theatres and festivals around the UK and overseas. Over a million copies of his poetry books and anthologies for Macmillan have been sold. Find out more about him at: **www.brianmoses.co.uk**

Roger Stevens is a children's author and poet who visits schools, libraries and festivals performing and running workshops. Roger also runs the Poetry Zone, a website for children and teachers: **www.poetryzone.co.uk**

Other books by Brian Moses and Roger Stevens

100% Unofficial! Olympic Poems
Brian Moses and Roger Stevens

A Cat Called Elvis
Brilliant poems by Brian Moses

Beware! Low Flying Rabbits
Poems by Roger Stevens

The Truth About Parents
*Hilarious rhymes by Paul Cookson, David Harmer,
Brian Moses and Roger Stevens*

The Truth About Teachers
*Hilarious rhymes by Paul Cookson, David Harmer,
Brian Moses and Roger Stevens*

What Are We Fighting For?

Illustrated by
Nicola L. Robinson

NEW POEMS ABOUT WAR

BRIAN MOSES AND ROGER STEVENS

MACMILLAN CHILDREN'S BOOKS

First published 2014 by Macmillan Children's Books
a division of Macmillan Publishers Limited
20 New Wharf Road, London N1 9RR
Basingstoke and Oxford
Associated companies throughout the world
www.panmacmillan.com

ISBN 978-1-4472-4861-3

A CIP catalogue record for this book is available from
the British Library.

Printed and bound by CPI Group (UK) Ltd, Croydon CR0 4YY

To the memory of both my father, Harry Moses, whose 'During the war . . .' stories I often failed to appreciate as a child, and my father-in-law, John Joseph Ford, who, at fifteen years old, ran away from home to join the army.

(BM)

For my father, Tom Stevens, who drove a tank in the Second World War and told me the story of tanks passing by, and my father-in-law, Roy Pryor, who was in the Royal Army Medical Corps and was captured at Dunkirk, and who still tells me what life was like as a prisoner of war.

(RS)

Contents

The First World War

'Swear by the green of the spring that you'll never forget'

Siegfried Sassoon

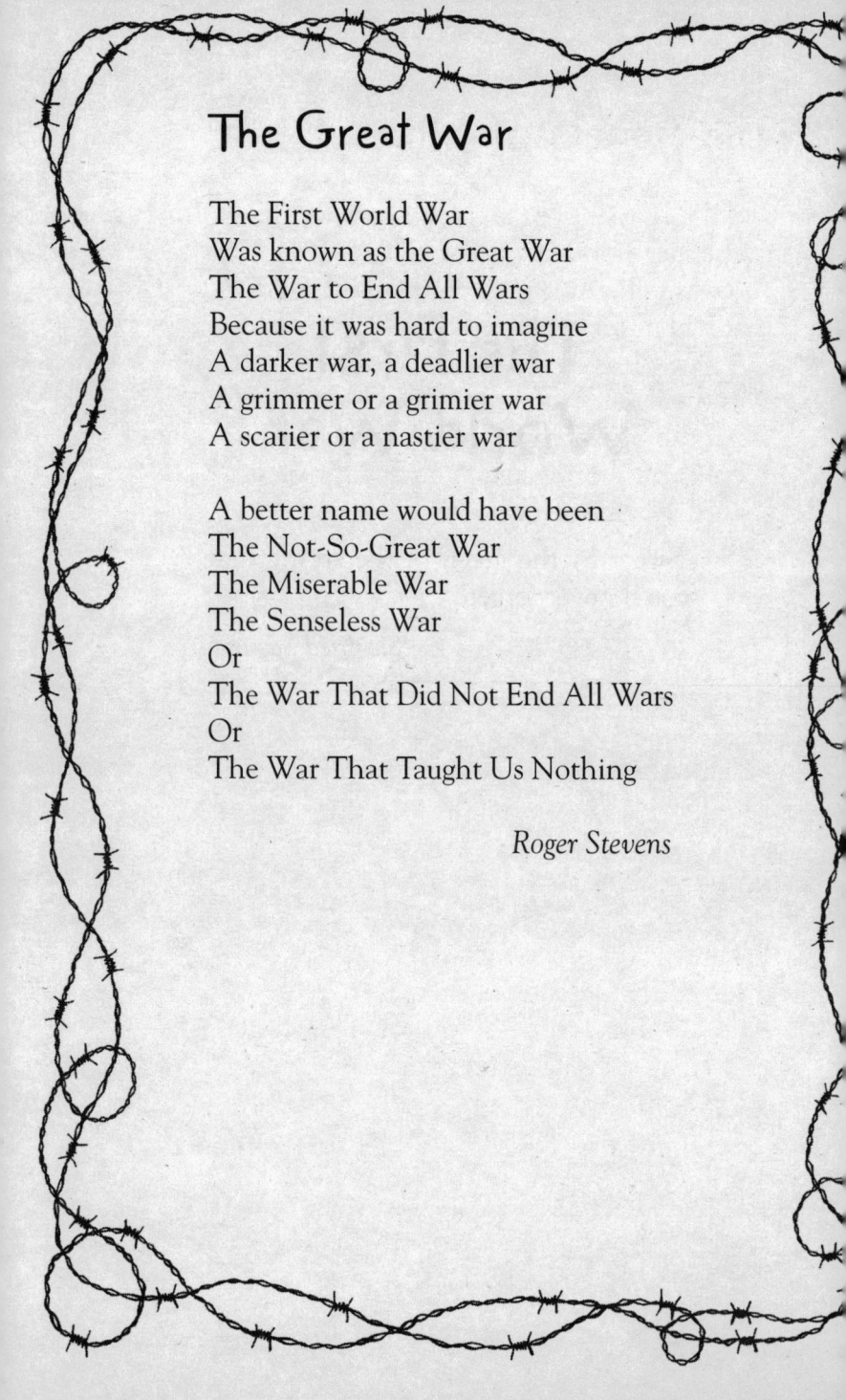

The Great War

The First World War
Was known as the Great War
The War to End All Wars
Because it was hard to imagine
A darker war, a deadlier war
A grimmer or a grimier war
A scarier or a nastier war

A better name would have been
The Not-So-Great War
The Miserable War
The Senseless War
Or
The War That Did Not End All Wars
Or
The War That Taught Us Nothing

Roger Stevens

The Angels of Mons

Did the British have divine protection
in the first months of the war,
and was something seen on the battlefield
that had never been seen before?

Was there really an army of angels
when the British thought they were beat?
Were there shining figures among the clouds
that protected the British retreat?

Was the German cavalry stopped in its tracks
as the horses refused to advance?
And was it a supernatural sight
that gave the British a chance?

Some say that it was spectral figures
with flaming swords that lit the night.
Others say bowmen fired arrows
tipped with bright pulsating light.

Whatever happened soldiers escaped
when really they should have died.
And the Angels of Mons showed British troops
that Heaven could be on their side.

Brian Moses

*Some British soldiers claimed to have seen visions in the sky while
retreating after the Battle of Mons, August 1914.*

Smile Please

I saw some old newsreels
Of the Great War

And I saw young men
From the towns and villages of Britain
Smiling for the cameras
Smiles as wide as sunshine
Like they were going on holiday

But as the French winter set in
And the mud in the trenches
Got thicker and colder

And more of their friends died
From bullet wounds
From explosions
From poisonous gas

The young men
Wading up to their waists in freezing mud
Tending the wounded and the dying
Were no longer smiling for the cameras

I saw some old newsreels
Of the Great War
And wondered
What were we fighting for?

Roger Stevens

The General's Message on the Morning of Battle

It's a beautiful day for a battle,
the sun is shining bright,
birds are high in the sky,
it's a lovely day for a fight.

God is on our side, lads,
he's sure to help us win.
We're fighting the good fight,
impatient to begin.

The war will soon be over,
the war will soon be won.
We just need one more push to
help us rout the Hun.

Good luck to every one of you,
play up and play the game,
we've beaten them at football
and again we'll do the same.

So come on lads, do your duty,
it's over the top you go.
I'll be with you there in spirit
as you race to meet the foe.

Our enemy is weakened,
we're sure to have them beat.
But just in case we don't,
I'll be leading the retreat!

Brian Moses

The Hun – First World War slang for German soldiers

Christmas Truce

'Hey, Tommy, you like tobacco?'
'Hey, Fritz, have my bottle of beer.'
'It's Christmas Day,
goodwill to all men, so,
what are we doing here?'

And maybe it would have stopped
then and there, once Tommy and Fritz had realized
that both were ordinary men.
That both had families,
girlfriends, wives,
that both were a long, long way
from anywhere anyone
called home.

And all that sad, strange Christmas Day,
Tommy and Fritz shook hands with each other,
sang together the Christmas songs
that both discovered they knew.
They joked with each other
through gestures and signs,
in a language that needed
no words.

Then a football was found
and they played a match,
two nations in the midst
of war, the score unimportant.

And it finished with a rifle shot
that sent men back to their dugouts.
Shouts of, 'Merry Christmas, Tommy,'
and, 'Happy New Year to you, Fritz.'
'Meet you again tomorrow,
show you photos of my girl.'

But it wouldn't do
for the guns to stay silent
or to think of your enemy
as a friend.

The rules of war
are clearly defined,
and someone must win
in the end.

Brian Moses

Tommy – First World War slang for British soldiers
Fritz – First World War slang for German soldiers

Home by Christmas

Victor watched as his dad
chained his bike to a tree
then waved goodbye
as he went to war.

Home by Christmas,
everyone said.
By then the war will be won,
the danger gone.

'I'll have had an adventure
in a foreign land,
something to tell grandchildren
in years to come,'
his dad had told him.

'We'll be welcomed back like heroes,
dancing in Trafalgar Square,
celebrating with our loved ones.
We'll be safe, alive and well.

'And no, it won't be dangerous,
we won't be there for long.
Just watch the lane,
I'll be riding back,
you'll hardly know
that I've gone.'

And all Victor wanted
was his dad to be home for Christmas lunch,
for the war to be over and won.

But sadly all Victor could see
was an empty place at the table,
a bike still chained to a tree.

Brian Moses

*When the First World War began in August 1914, most British
families thought it would all be over by Christmas. Unfortunately,
the war continued until November 1918.*

Big Bertha

Gustav Krupp
Fancy naming your wonder gun
After your wife
'Big Bertha'

I wonder how she felt about that?

Maybe she was proud
Of her husband
Who had designed a gun
That could fire a two thousand and fifty pound shell
Over nine miles

She probably didn't consider
The damage it might have done
Or the deaths it caused
There was a war on after all.

I wonder if she was a large woman
Big Bertha?

Or maybe she simply had
A big explosive personality?

Roger Stevens

Dear Mum

If you receive this letter
I'll be gone
To who knows where?
To Heaven, I hope.
So please don't cry.
And give my love to Lop,
Our cat who lost his tail.
And Dad, of course.
I hope that this year's crop
Of spuds do well.

And give my love to Ruth
I know I promised her
That we would marry in the spring
But tell her that I love her
(And you
And Dad
And Lop, the cat).

I have to go
The big offensive's come
Don't worry, Mum
Oh, and please give Ruth
This ring.

From John
Your ever-loving son

Roger Stevens

Goodbye Note

I'm saying goodbye to England,
from a trench somewhere in France.
Saying goodbye to my girl
and our fun at the Saturday dance.

Goodbye family farm,
goodbye house on the hill,
goodbye to the fields,
the river and the gill.

Goodbye to the silence,
the solitude and the peace,
goodbye to home-baked scones
and my mother's family feast.

Goodbye to the hens I tended,
goodbye to my dog and my mouse,
to the cows at rest in the byre,
to the swallows that circle our house.

A fond goodbye to my school,
where I was taught the recourse
to settle any argument
was words, and never force.

Till here with the rattle of gunfire,
the bayonets, the blood,
the wounded and the dying,
the screaming and the mud.

There's little chance that I'll escape
a bullet or a shell,
I'm saying goodbye to all I love
and saying hello to Hell.

Brian Moses

Gill – narrow stream through a wooded ravine
Byre – stable

Soldiers in the trenches would often keep a letter to
their loved ones on their person before they went into
battle, to be sent home if they died.

The Colour of
Your Skin

You would have thought
That in a war
The colour of your skin
Would make no difference

But in the Great War
Only white American soldiers
Were allowed
To die in glory

The Harlem Hellfighters
So brave they would have faced the Devil himself
Won the Croix de Guerre

But returned to America to find
Their deeds of heroism
Ignored

Today you might find this story
Hard to believe

Roger Stevens

*Croix de Guerre – medal awarded by the French government to soldiers
who fought for France during both world wars. More than 200,000 African-
Americans served in the First World War. The majority of men worked in
labour divisions although about eleven per cent fought in combat forces. They
served in segregated divisions (the 92nd and 93rd) and trained separately.*

When Your Name's Not on the List

Every week
The names
Of the dead
And missing
Are pinned up
On the church noticeboard

And Mum
Gives me a lovely safe squeeze
Because Dad's name
Is not there

Roger Stevens

Somme

In the Battle of the Somme
First of July
Nineteen sixteen
Over nineteen thousand soldiers died
And half a million fell

And fighting with the French
Young Canadians, Australians, Bermudians and Indians
Newfoundlanders, New Zealanders
South Africans and British
Joined the Germans in that hell

One hundred years on
In the green and pleasant Somme
You'd hardly know there'd been a war
But for the story that the nineteen thousand poppies
Tell

Roger Stevens

Tipperary

'It's a long way to Tipperary, it's a long way to go . . .'

It was almost *his* song,
'Tipperary'.
His parents' farm five miles from town.
Tipperary, the place
they drove cows to market.

And all it took
was the babble of rooks
in the yew trees of French villages,
the smell of wild garlic
on the breeze at night,
and he was there,
Tipperary.

'It's a long, long way to tickle Mary,'
they sang on marches.

And Mary was the name
for every girl they'd left behind.
But not him.

Sixteen, never been kissed,
enlisted illegally.
Trumpets, fanfare,
bit of a dare really.

Till two years on and war-weary,
eyes closed, sun on his face,
he'd think himself there.

'It's a long long way to Tipperary,'
he'd hum.

Till opening his eyes he'd discover
how far it was
and always would be.

Brian Moses

The Nation at Home

At first, the nation at home hardly knew there
    was a war on.
There were no TVs transmitting the news into
    every sitting room.
No mobile phones sending video footage live
    from the front.
No satellites beaming back images of troop
    movements.
No tweeters on Twitter.
No way you could Google the Somme.
They hardly knew there was a war on,
knew nothing of the terror, bayonets
    charging machine guns.
Till one day the newspapers showed
    soldiers stumbling from trains.
The walking wounded, bloodied
    and dazed,
bringing the war back home.

Brian Moses

Trench Warfare

the sTench of death
in the cRowded trenches
breathing smokE and hot ash, the rattle of
machine guNs, animals struggling to
haul the heavy Cannons through the mud
and the terrified Horses strain, stumble
while we are up to our Waists in freezing water and muck
the whistle blows! Attack! we say a hurried prayer
we scramble oveR the top, across barbed wire
so many Friends fall, retreat
only the deAd can escape this hell
and for yeaRs the living dream of
explosions, I wakE up shaking and scared

Roger Stevens

Abandoned Dog

Abandoned dog
found wandering in no-man's-land.
A Labrador bitch
or something like it,
coal-scuttle black.
Chalky saw it, kept calling.
His family had dogs
before the war, a dozen or so
in a farmhouse
on the North York Moors.
The dog didn't trust him at first
but he offered food
and she must have been starving.
Came back each night,
lucky she wasn't shot.
Then one time she stayed,
played with Chalky.

He knew the right place
to stroke her,
to keep her calm.
You could tell she'd been through hell,
every noise spooked her.
Chalky understood, eased her
beneath his blanket.
'Lucky' he named her.
Lucky for him too,
as a gentle rhythm, heart against heart,
brought both the stillness they needed.

Brian Moses

*During the First World War, some dogs were trained to
take messages from one part of the battlefield to another.
Other dogs were abandoned by their owners and were
stranded in the middle of a battle as the front lines advanced.*

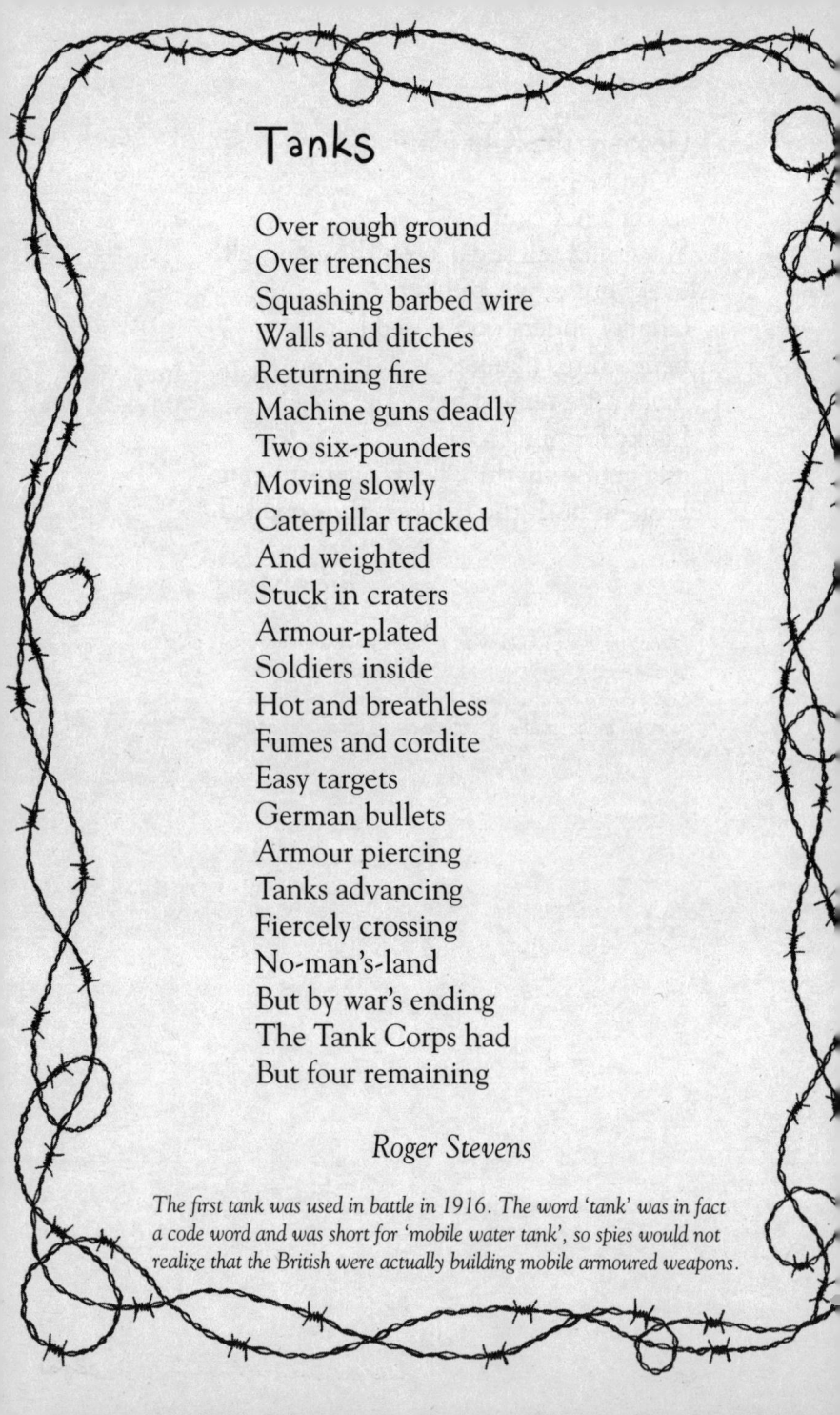

Tanks

Over rough ground
Over trenches
Squashing barbed wire
Walls and ditches
Returning fire
Machine guns deadly
Two six-pounders
Moving slowly
Caterpillar tracked
And weighted
Stuck in craters
Armour-plated
Soldiers inside
Hot and breathless
Fumes and cordite
Easy targets
German bullets
Armour piercing
Tanks advancing
Fiercely crossing
No-man's-land
But by war's ending
The Tank Corps had
But four remaining

Roger Stevens

The first tank was used in battle in 1916. The word 'tank' was in fact a code word and was short for 'mobile water tank', so spies would not realize that the British were actually building mobile armoured weapons.

Luke and Jessie

Luke was nineteen when he died.
His gravestone gives no information
about where or how and signals just one of a million
    deaths that year.
His fiancée Jessie was sixteen when the news came
    back, along with her photo from his tunic pocket
    where he'd kept her close to his heart.
The love of her life,
she grieved his passing, never quite found
anyone else who triggered the feelings she had
    for her soldier boy.
She visited his grave, laid flowers.
She grew old,
as he never did.
One hundred years when she died, knowing again
    she'd be with him. Together then, together now,
for eternity.

Brian Moses

*Private Luke Leadbetter was killed in 1917. His grave can be seen in the
Aeroplane Cemetery near Ypres. His fiancée Jessie arranged for her ashes to
be laid on his grave when she died eighty-four years later.*

Pals

Harry and Spud, Rawlings and I,
we were pals.
We lived in the same street,
attended the same school.

When war broke out
we joined up.
Seemed right somehow,
the four of us, together,
doing our bit
for King and Country.

It was hard at first,
but there were laughs too.
Harry and Spud, Rawlings and I
helped each other through.

We sang the songs,
not tunefully, but
enthusiastically.
I remember Spud
serenading Harry:
'If you were the only girl
in the world,' he warbled,
till Harry thumped him.

And laughter was the key
to keep our spirits up
when all we had
to look forward to
was mud and blood and bullets.

No idea why I survived
and they didn't.
One of the lucky ones
me, kept my head
below the parapet
and somehow the bullets
passed me by.

I've lived in the same street
all my life, and every year the wife
and I stand here on Remembrance Day
while I say a prayer for Harry and Spud
and Rawlings.

I run my fingers
over the names, etched in stone,
remember where their lives were lost,
and how we won the war,
but at what cost?

Brian Moses

Conscientious Objector

Nineteen sixteen and half a million dead
Volunteers thin on the ground and the
    government said
Now you have to fight

But Danny Jones had read the Bible
Love your enemies, Jesus said
Fighting isn't right

So Danny joined the Red Cross
Stretchered the wounded through the trenches
In the dying light

And what he saw, no man should see
So do not question Danny's bravery
When he refused to fight

Roger Stevens

Bravery

After Adrian Mitchell

Over the top
In the face of enemy fire
Bravery
I like that stuff

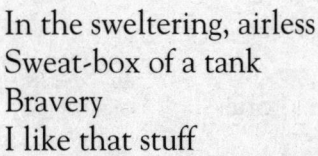

In the sweltering, airless
Sweat-box of a tank
Bravery
I like that stuff

In the sky above the fields of France
Enemy planes coming out of the sun
Bravery
I like that stuff

Defusing a bomb, rescuing
A child from a firebombed house
Bravery
I like that stuff

Fighting, fighting, killing, wounding, maiming
All for a piece of land?
War
I hate that stuff

Roger Stevens

Pip, Squeak and Wilfred

Rummaging in the attic
I found a rusty OXO tin
With three medals in
Grandma said
The bronze Mons Star
Has her dad's name on the back

The British War Medal shines silver
St George, sword raised
Trampling the enemy's skull and bones

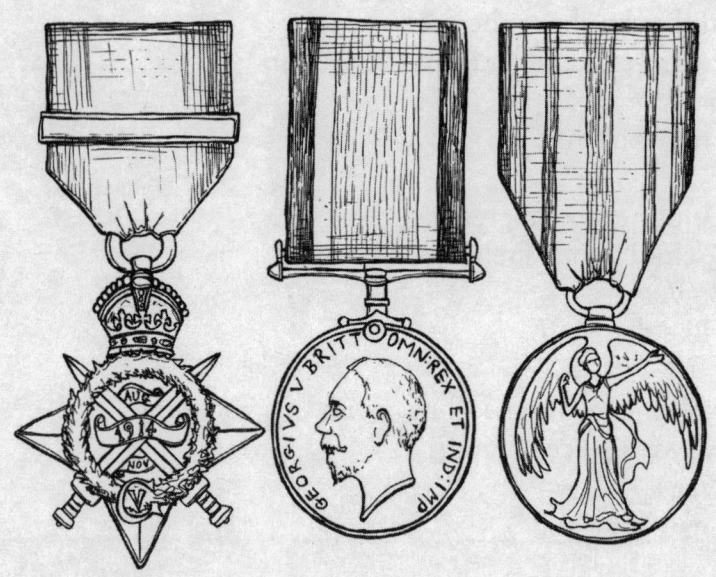

The Victory Medal weighs heavy
And Winged Victory stretches out her arm
A goddess claiming all the world as her own
And on the back
The Great War for Civilisation

Grandma said they were nicknamed
Pip, Squeak and Wilfred
After a cartoon family of orphaned animals
In a *Daily Mirror* cartoon strip

Pip the dog
Squeak the penguin
And Wilfred the long-eared rabbit

Almost everyone won a medal
Grandma said.
If you survived that war
You deserved it

Roger Stevens

Cenotaph

Grandma
Told me about her dad
How he'd comb his hair
Wear his Sunday suit
(Only once a year
He'd wear a tie)
To make that long, slow walk
   to the Cenotaph
On a dark and chilly November
   morning
His medals polished
And pinned to the front
   pocket
To remember all those
   soldiers and friends
Who fell
Who never won a medal
Who never made it to
   December

Roger Stevens

*A cenotaph is a monument used as a
memorial to honour a person or group
of people whose remains are elsewhere.*

THE GLORIOUS DEAD

The Second World War

'Never in the field of human conflict was so much owed by so many to so few'

Winston Churchill on the Battle of Britain

3rd September 1939

It seemed as if
it was just another ordinary Sunday.
Looking back I recall that
Mum and Dad were quieter than usual,
kept exchanging looks that they thought
we didn't notice. The cat was fed
then brushed herself against my legs.
There were eggs for breakfast
as there always were on Sunday.
Mum didn't eat much and we thought
perhaps she wasn't feeling well.
We could tell there was something
the matter. Dad snapped at us,
said to eat, not chatter. So we did,
Billy and me, then kicked at each other
under the table. 'Ow!' Billy yelled.
'That hurt.'
'You'll both have something
to yell about, if you keep that up,'
Dad warned.
'Go on,' he said,
'get out of our sight.'

An hour later we tiptoed back.
The house was quiet except
for the radio's crackle, and then
a sombre voice spoke the words
that nobody wanted to hear:
'This country is at war
with Germany.'

Brian Moses

Evacuation

I dunno why Mum's crying so
We'll be fine
Got on the train to Wales
My sister and me
And a hundred other children
Heading for the sunshine
Although we don't know
Exactly where we're going
I've got a label though
So I won't get lost
The government said
We had to go
And we'll be safe, away from the bombs
And anyway it will be exciting
All that space to play in
And hills to climb
And sheep to chase
So I don't know why Mum's crying

Roger Stevens

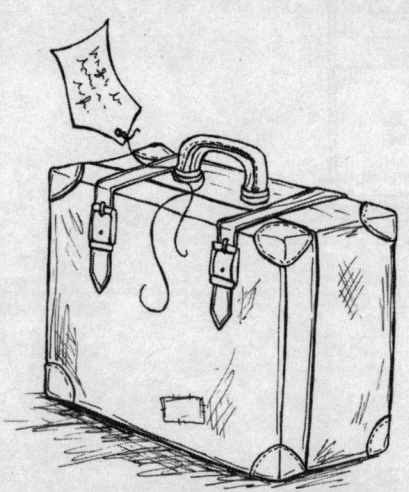

Mollie

It was fine, all the time
she had Mollie,
as much as a rough sea and
a bucking boat could ever be really fine.
Leaving Guernsey, that feeling
of being lonely, but not alone,
with friends, but not family.
She'd always travelled with her parents before
and now she'd left them behind.

So she clutched the doll, held her close,
tried to smile, tried to eat something,
to look on the bright side, as Mum would say,
put a brave face on it.
But somewhere between the ship and the train,
on the rainy streets of Weymouth,
in the hustle and bustle of a hurried chase
to reach the station on time,
Mollie must have fallen from her pocket.

It wasn't till the train hissed and set off
that she realized Mollie was missing.
Her teacher's hugs, her soft voice,
the sympathy of her friends,
nothing could console her, the tears
ran fast and freely.

And in the hours and hours it took
for the train to steam its way north,
the loss of the doll seemed
a link in a chain, now broken.
She and her family driven apart.
They, still in danger on Guernsey,
while she journeyed on to find
a new home with strangers.

Brian Moses

*Parents in the Channel Islands had to choose between
keeping their children with them or sending them to
the British mainland. Many children faced a long sea
crossing followed by an even longer train journey to
the north of England.*

Letter from Two Elderly Ladies Who Volunteered to Do Their Bit and Help the War Effort by Taking in Evacuees

Dear Sir, -

We'd like to swap our evacuees,
*   we don't like the ones we've got! They're*
messy and they're smelly, they've got lice
and they swear a lot.
*   We thought we'd be getting children who*
knew how to be polite,
*   who didn't fight all the time and could*
tell wrong from right.
*   We thought they'd be kind and grateful*
for the food we give them to eat,
*   but they seem to ignore the vegetables*
and only eat the meat.
*   The chickens have stopped laying eggs*
they're chasing them everywhere.
*   The cat just won't come near them since*
they pulled out tufts of his hair.
*   It isn't Christian we know,*
*   but we just can't take any more. Every*
day the neighbours
*   come knocking on our door.*
*   So can we swap our evacuees? I'm sure*

they don't like us. We're sorry to have to ask,
   it's not like us to make a fuss.

Yours faithfully,

Lizzie & Florence Abercrombie

Brian Moses

Another War

It wasn't just a war between the Germans and the Brits
it was a war between the vackies and the village kids.

It was a war of words, a war of stones,
it was a war that threatened broken bones.

It was village kids with faces of granite
as if they belonged to some other planet.

'Go back home, we don't want you here,
go back where you came from, disappear.'

It wasn't just a war between the Germans and the Brits
it was a war between the vackies and the village kids.

It was 'us and them', it was 'them and us',
it was mud fights causing family fuss.

Kids were rolling around in the dirt,
thumping each other and getting hurt.

Bloody noses and cauliflower ears,
the noise of jeering and lusty cheers.

It wasn't just a war between the Germans and the Brits
it was a war between the vackies and the village kids.

It was big 'uns bullying and little 'uns crying,
it was twisted arms and fists that were flying.

It was, 'See you later for a fight after school!'
and, 'Chicken if you don't show, that's the rule.'

'You vackies will regret ever leaving your town
because we're the gang here and we'll knock you
     down.'

And it wasn't just a war between the Germans and the
*   Brits*
it was a war between the vackies and the village kids,
it was a war between the vackies and the village kids.

Brian Moses

Rude Noises

It winds our teacher up
when we make rude noises
through our gas masks.

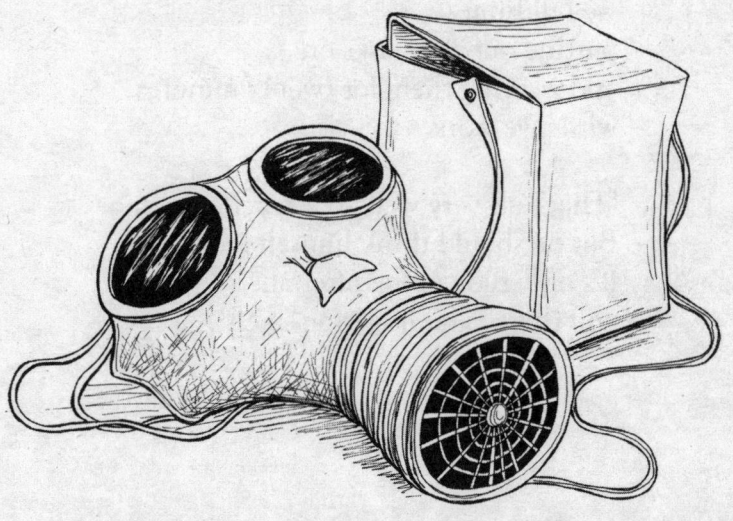

We take it in turns
to breathe out quickly
till the rubber vibrates
and the noise escapes.

Then if we're feeling
that he deserves
some real aggravation,
we start up our
rude-noise orchestra.

We find it amusing,
we find it fun,
but he seems to have lost
his sense of humour.

'We're meant to practise every day,'
we tell him,
putting our gas masks on
and wearing them for twenty minutes
while we work.

'That's all very well,' our teacher says.
But he should think himself lucky,
it's only rude noises after all,
and there is no lingering smell!

Brian Moses

No Surrender

'There will be no surrender.'

It was a statement from Winnie in a stern and
    passionate speech.
It was scrawled in vapour trails on a canvas of sky
    above Kent.
It was the man in the rubble that once was his
    home, shaking his fist at the sky.
It was soldiers defiant on Dunkirk's beaches wading
    out to warships.
It was Auntie Doris pounding a pub piano while
    the sirens sounded.
It was 'There'll Always Be an England', 'Rule,
    Britannia!' and 'Jerusalem'.
It was eyes filling with tears at the sight of the flag.

'There will be no surrender.'

And there wasn't.

Brian Moses

*'Winnie' was the affectionate name for Winston Churchill, Britain's Prime
Minister for most of the Second World War.*

Photograph

Here's the photo I took
Last year on the beach
Dad wearing the tie
I bought him for his birthday
Billy drinking lemonade
The straw up his nose
And Mum huddled up in her coat
Against the seaside wind

Now Dad's in France
And our beach is covered in concrete
And tangled barbed wire
And landmines
In case the Germans invade

But on that day
We'd just made
The world's grandest sandcastle
And watched the tide
Rush in
Filling the moat
Gradually washing
It all away

Roger
Stevens

The Little Ships

Dunkirk, June 1940

We helped rescue the British Army,
my dad, the *Mayflower* and me.

We were one of those little ships
in a flotilla that put to sea.

We took on-board the soldiers
left stranded on the beaches of France.

When destroyers couldn't reach them
we were able to advance.

Beneath a hail of bullets
that rained down on the sea,

we helped rescue the British Army,
my dad, the *Mayflower* and me.

Brian Moses

During the Battle of Dunkirk, hundreds of thousands of Allied soldiers were trapped between the German Army and the sea in Dunkirk, France. To help evacuate the soldiers, hundreds of small fishing vessels and lifeboats were called into action alongside the British Navy, rescuing over 300,000 troops.

Safe

'We'll be safe,' I heard Dad say,
'from all but a direct hit.'

Safe, I thought, how can we
be safe?
Already we're buried
under two feet of earth,
Dad's cabbages growing on top.

Already it feels
as if we're in our tomb,
in this shelter we sleep in
each night.

Hearing the crump
of explosions,
like giant's footsteps
shaking the ground
and edging closer.

I have a life worth living
and I will survive,
I tell myself.

But how on earth did I think
that war might be fun,
tucked beneath the ground
like rabbits in a burrow?

'If a bomb's got our name on it . . .'
I heard Mum say to Dad,
and although she never
finished the sentence,
I knew what she meant.

But was it right, I wondered,
to hope that a bomb
had someone else's name
on it?

Brian Moses

Night after Night after Night

I remember the wailing sirens, the hurried waking,
the stumbling down the street with blankets
in our arms and pushing our way into the shelter.
I remember the dog howling from the house
when we weren't allowed to take her with us.
I remember the interrupted nights,
my bedroom, the shelter, then back in my bed again.
I remember the anger of the guns as they desperately
    tried
to turn back the bombers or throw them off target.
I remember the whistle and whine of the bombs that
    fell,
the fear that the nearest explosion could have been
    our house.
I remember the all-clear, the peering from the doorway
to see if the street had suffered, if the houses still stood.
I remember the men raking through the wreckage,
the relief that our house had its doors and
    windows intact.
I remember the dust and the smoke from the
    fires that still burned.
I remember thinking, does it even the score,
    if we do the same
to German cities? Will it help *us* win this war?

Brian Moses

*During the Blitz in 1940, London was bombed for fifty-seven nights in a row.
Over a million homes were damaged or destroyed and more than 40,000
Londoners died.*

A Message to Adolf

When photographs were published of Londoners,
they were never looking gloomy or depressed,
never looking fed up or exhausted
or wearied by the nightly lack of rest.

The mood was always one of optimism,
bombed out we may be but we're not down.
We'll do anything to keep our spirits up,
show everyone a smile and not a frown.

We can take it, so Hitler do your worst,
you're mistaken if you think that you can win.
All that you can do will never be enough:
the British people will never give in.

Brian Moses

*Newspapers were discouraged from showing too many pictures of bomb
damage or people looking unhappy, injured or depressed.*

Airmen

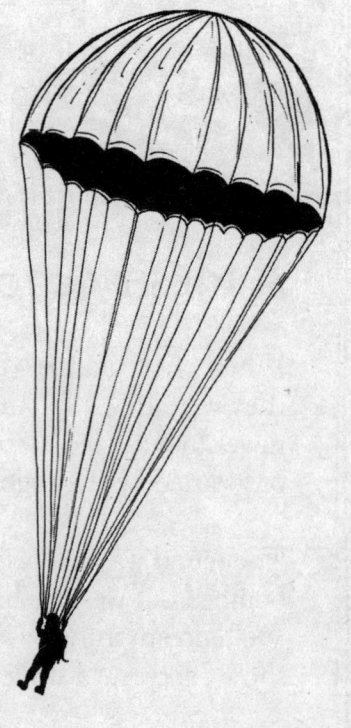

As the sun set
We watched the plane
Spiral out of control
Heard the clump
As it hit the ground
Beyond the wood

Saw the thin plume of smoke
Grey, laced with pink
Rising above the crash
Like a question mark
Then we saw the parachute
Caught in the sun
Like a drifting star
And that night in bed
I listened to the whistles
As they searched the wood
For that German airman

I imagined him being frightened
Far from home
And I pulled my eiderdown
Around me
And thought of Dad
And offered up a prayer
For lonely airmen
Everywhere

Roger Stevens

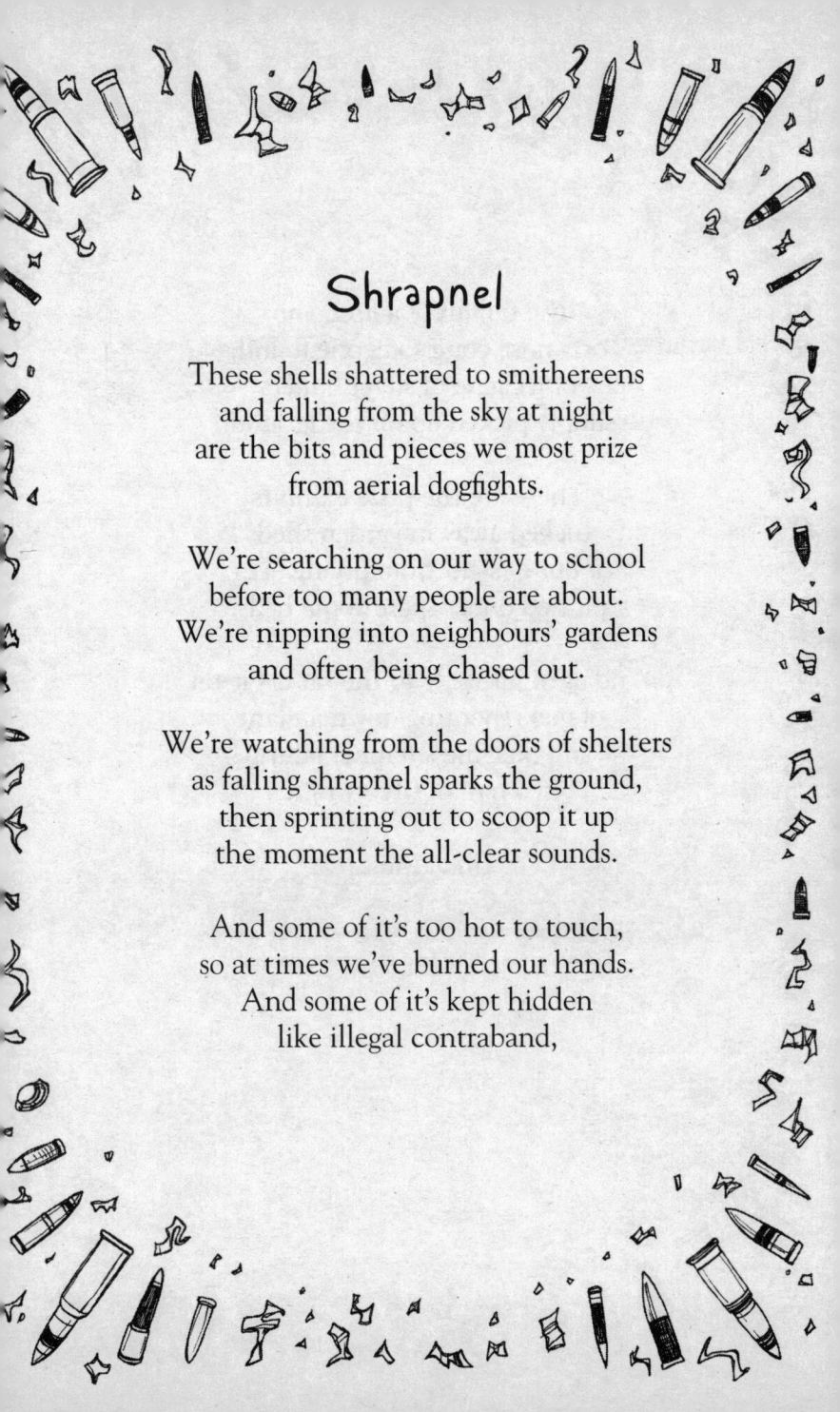

Shrapnel

These shells shattered to smithereens
and falling from the sky at night
are the bits and pieces we most prize
from aerial dogfights.

We're searching on our way to school
before too many people are about.
We're nipping into neighbours' gardens
and often being chased out.

We're watching from the doors of shelters
as falling shrapnel sparks the ground,
then sprinting out to scoop it up
the moment the all-clear sounds.

And some of it's too hot to touch,
so at times we've burned our hands.
And some of it's kept hidden
like illegal contraband,

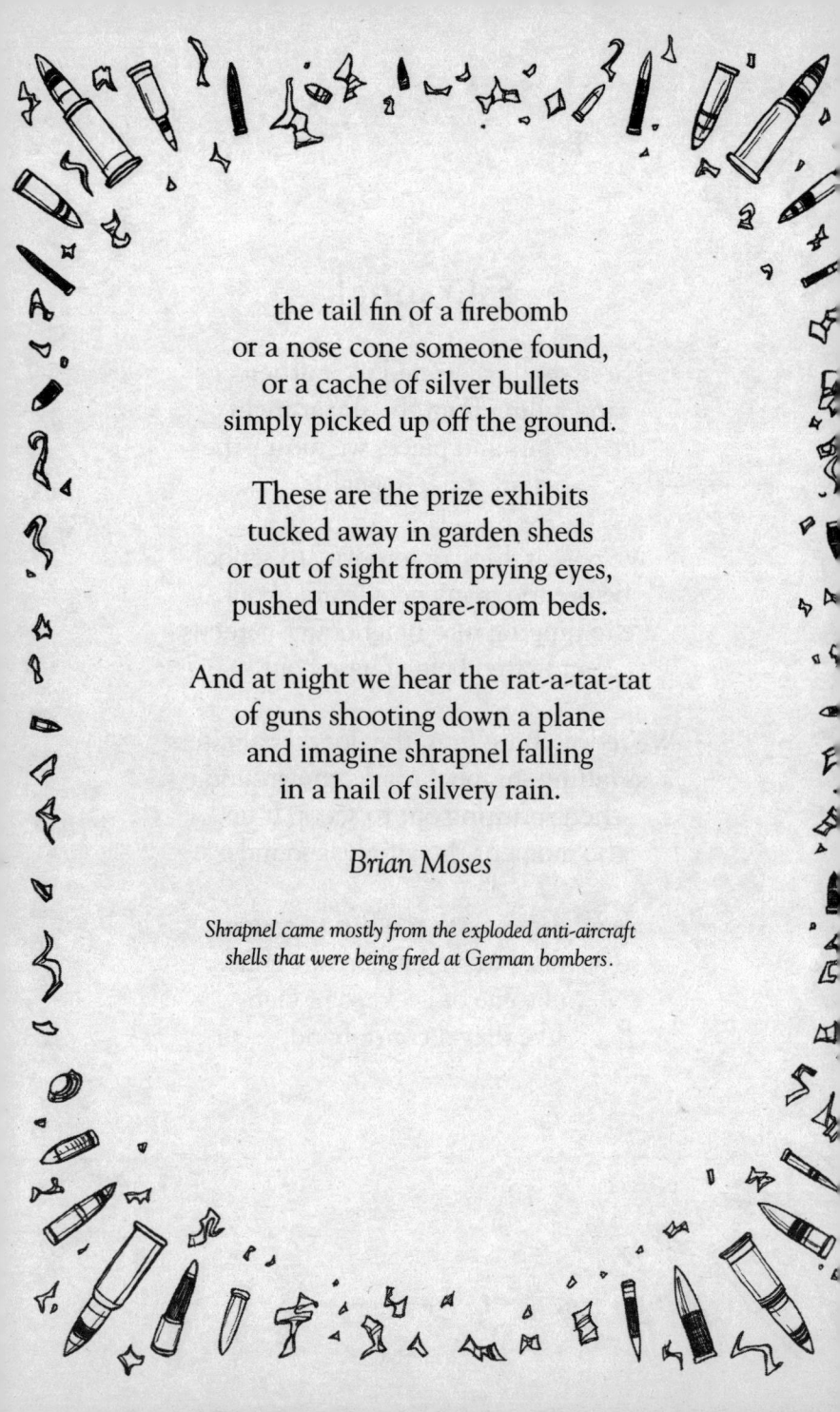

the tail fin of a firebomb
or a nose cone someone found,
or a cache of silver bullets
simply picked up off the ground.

These are the prize exhibits
tucked away in garden sheds
or out of sight from prying eyes,
pushed under spare-room beds.

And at night we hear the rat-a-tat-tat
of guns shooting down a plane
and imagine shrapnel falling
in a hail of silvery rain.

Brian Moses

*Shrapnel came mostly from the exploded anti-aircraft
shells that were being fired at German bombers.*

Eating Carrots

It's why we need to eat carrots,
Mum says,
so we can see in the blackout.

But I remember reading
in the *Boys' Book of Knowledge*
how it would take a lifetime
of eating carrots,
and not just a few, but thousands,
to make a real difference.

Mum doesn't listen,
she won't see sense.
She cooks carrot tart, carrot flan,
carrot mash, carrot jam,
carrot cake, carrot surprise (it never is!),
carrot chutney, carrot rissoles,
carrot pie, carrot sausages,
carrot jelly, carrot omelette,
carrot scones, carrot loaf,
carrot crumble, carrot sponge
and carrot marmalade.

Then she tells us
we'll notice a difference soon.

But the only time I can see
in the dark
is under the glow from
a friendly moon,
and it's still as black as it always was
in my blacked out room.

Brian Moses

*During the Second World War, the British government
spread propaganda saying that eating carrots would
help you to see in the dark. This was to cover up the
development of radar technology, which allowed British
pilots to pinpoint the location on enemy planes in the dark.*

Learner Drivers

A trail of smashed milk bottles
The pavement's milky wet
Billy's football squashed and burst
Billy's quite upset

Mrs Jones's geraniums
Fit for the compost heap
Mum's vase bounced off the sideboard
You should have seen it leap

And Grandad's bicycle's been crushed
He's in a proper fix
And the wall where Grandad leaned his bike
Is now a pile of bricks

Three lamp posts bent like coat hangers
Our cat has run away
You have to learn to drive a tank
And the lessons were today

Roger Stevens

Sweets

The government says
I can only have
two ounces of **sweets**
a week.

That's far too few
so all day through
I constantly dream
of **sweets**.

Forget 'Doctor Carrot'
and 'Potato Pete'.
What will do me good
is a bag of **sweets**.

I smile charmingly
at Americans I meet,
'Got any gum, chum?'
I need **sweets**.

It isn't right
that **sweets** are on ration.
It's sugar I need,
sweets are my passion.

I'm pleading with you
for kids everywhere.
Give us our **sweets**,
it just isn't fair.

I know that in war
we must smile and make do,
but a few extra toffees
or another chew

wouldn't hurt the war effort,
surely not,
and for all us kids
it would mean a lot!

But the government says
our ration is enough;
for MPs maybe
but for kids, it's tough.

Brian Moses

*Two ounces is equal to fifty-seven grams,
about the same weight as eight two-pence pieces.*

Women's Work

Building bridges
Making fences
Searchlight, ack-ack
Air defences
Air-raid wardens
Taking chances
Driving cars
And ambulances
Fixing cars
Changing tyres
Electricians
Changing wires
Fire brigade
To put out fires
Eighty thousand
On the farms
In factories
Making arms
Making uniforms
And boots
Carefully packing
Parachutes

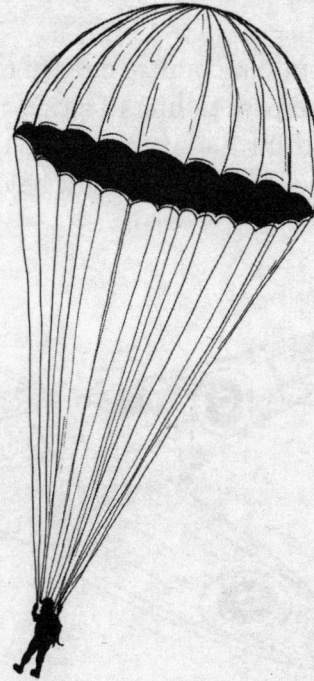

Of all the jobs
That men back then
Thought only men could do
Not unsurprisingly
It turned out, women
Could do them too.

Roger Stevens

*Before the Second World War, women were expected
to be housewives, secretaries, nurses or shop assistants.
But when men were called upon to fight, women were
called upon to fill their jobs, many of which were
previously thought to be unsuitable for women.*

Salvage

They told us our country needed metal
from a large park railing to a tiny tin kettle,
that everything had its place in a chain
and when melted down might be used in a plane.

So we made our collections, buckets and cans,
old metal baths, wheels from go-carts and prams,
my tin soldiers, the pot for our stew,
our kettle, a spade and an old horseshoe.

And it pleased us to think that all those things
might one day be part of a Spitfire's wings,
and that we would wonder which bit of metal
might previously have been our tin kettle.

Brian Moses

My Father's War

My father was a male nurse in the Royal Army Medical Corps
in the Second World War

My father fought his desert war,
picked up and patched up casualties.
It didn't matter what side they were on,
a wounded man was a wounded man,
Tunisia through to Italy.

In makeshift tents he spent his nights
with dying men, fighting his war on war,
winning back hope for the ones who felt
they'd lost everything, who glimpsed
in the owl-faced nurse a confessor, a friend.

Death dresses soldiers alike
in uniforms of ashen grey and white.
Those who died were quickly covered,
small mounds, a hymn, a prayer,
souls took wing to London or Berlin.

My father, in the grainy sepia snaps,
El Alamein through to Cassino,
then back by road across Europe,
glimpses of war-damaged towns
through gaps in a lorry's canvas flaps.

Over the years he blocked the horror,
kept it to himself and shared instead
the friendship, the sightseeing,
his Christmas lunch in Austria,
his blessing from the Pope.

And I regret all those times I closed
my ears – should have realized instead
how he never gloried in what he'd done,
just retold his war; tried to understand
what would never be understood.

Brian Moses

The Women's Land Army

We could do with thousands more like you
Is what the poster said
We need crops to feed the troops
And wheat to make the bread
The men are all off fighting
What are you waiting for?
Join the Women's Land Army
And help us win the war

I joined in nineteen thirty-nine
For thirty bob a week
Growing peas and beans and carrots
Cabbages and leeks
I could wrestle a reluctant sheep
When shearing time was nigh
Milk a cow, collect the eggs
Muck out the horses and the sty

I could strip a tractor engine
From carburettor to the coil
I could park it on a sixpence
Change the spark plugs and the oil
Women working on the land
Could show the men a thing or two
I could shoot a rat from twenty yards
I was called 'Quick Draw McGrew'

We dug the land and sowed and hoed
And harvested the grain
For fifty hours a week we worked
In cold and frost and rain
And when the sun was shining
What fun it was to be
Helping the war effort
In the Women's Land Army

Roger Stevens

Thirty bob was slang for thirty shillings (£1.50 in today's money). In the past people earned less, but things also cost less. Today this would be the equivalent of earning £80 a week.

Wartime Food

Could you eat a wartime diet?
Would you enjoy the food they ate?
Dried eggs instead of fresh ones,
whale meat instead of steak?

Tinned snoek with nettle purée,
or a nasty potato-peel pie.
Coffee from acorns or parsnips
when there wasn't any to buy.

The sea could offer limpets,
like gum without the taste,
chewing them would leave your mouth
glued up like sticky paste.

Carrageen moss, a sort of seaweed,
mixed with milk could make blancmange,
and spider crabs when cooked
would certainly make you cringe.

Shredded sprouts, beetroot sandwiches,
a glass of raw swede juice,
Potatoes with pig's liver baked in a pie
and labelled 'Poor Man's Goose'.

Then finish with a cup of bramble tea
and be grateful you still survive.
Food may have been unpalatable
but at least it kept you alive.

Brian Moses

Snoek – a tinned variety of a fish from South Africa called barracouta

Foods such as carrageen moss and limpets were eaten in the Channel Islands towards the end of the German occupation, when there were extreme shortages of food.

The Animal Victoria Cross

And to Simon
Who served
On HMS *Amethyst*
Who survived cannon shell
Raised morale
And despite injury
Dealt very well
With an infestation of rats
We award
The Dickin Medal
For bravery
For being
An exceptionally cat-like
Cat.

Roger Stevens

*The Dickin Medal for animal bravery
was the animal equivalent of the
Victoria Cross. It was awarded to
thirty-two pigeons, eighteen dogs, three
horses and one cat.*

Pigeon

Percy is our last pigeon
And I often come up to the pigeon loft
For a chat

Now Dad's gone
Mum says
We'll not be having
Any more pigeons
When Percy finally leaves us

I tell our pigeon about Mary of Exeter
A pigeon who fought in the war
Well, not exactly fought

Mary brought secret messages home from France
She was shot down once, but still made it back
And once she was four days late
After an attack by a falcon
And once she was hit by shrapnel
But still got back in one piece
She had twenty-two stitches
And won the Dickin Medal

I wonder if Percy is jealous
Or is he pleased he missed it all?
Maybe I'm the jealous one

Jealous that Mary of Exeter
Made it back from the war
But Dad didn't

Roger Stevens

*After Mary's war service her owner made her a
leather collar to support her injured neck and head.
She lived until 1950 and was buried with full
military honours.*

Doodlebug

Look, there it is
A tiny speck in the sky, growing larger
Like some weird black beetle on the wing
Flying in a dead straight line

Listen, now you hear it
A drone
Like a disturbed wasp's nest
And growing louder
As it passes over

Sigh, with relief
Because if the drone stops
You run like hell
And hope you're you fast enough
To escape the doodlebug's
Deadly sting

Roger Stevens

Doodlebugs, also known as V-1 flying bombs, were an early kind of jet-propelled bomb. Their engines made a buzzing noise like a large insect. When the noise stopped, it meant the bomb was about to explode.

Miss Leaky Mouth

Miss Leaky Mouth will blab
so be careful what you say.
Don't try to confide in her,
don't give anything away.

She just can't keep her mouth shut,
she can't control her tongue.
Let her in on a secret
and she'll tell everyone.

In wartime walls have ears,
it's something we recognize.
That ordinary guy she's talking to
might well be in disguise.

Spies will be almost anywhere
and listen to anything.
Miss Leaky Mouth's a canary,
she'll open her mouth and sing.

Her lips are loose so never say
what you wouldn't want repeated.
Careless talk costs lives (it's true)
and we could be defeated.

Brian Moses

*Miss Leaky Mouth was a cartoon character in the Second
World War, warning everyone about the danger of giving
information to strangers, in case they turned out to be enemy spies.*

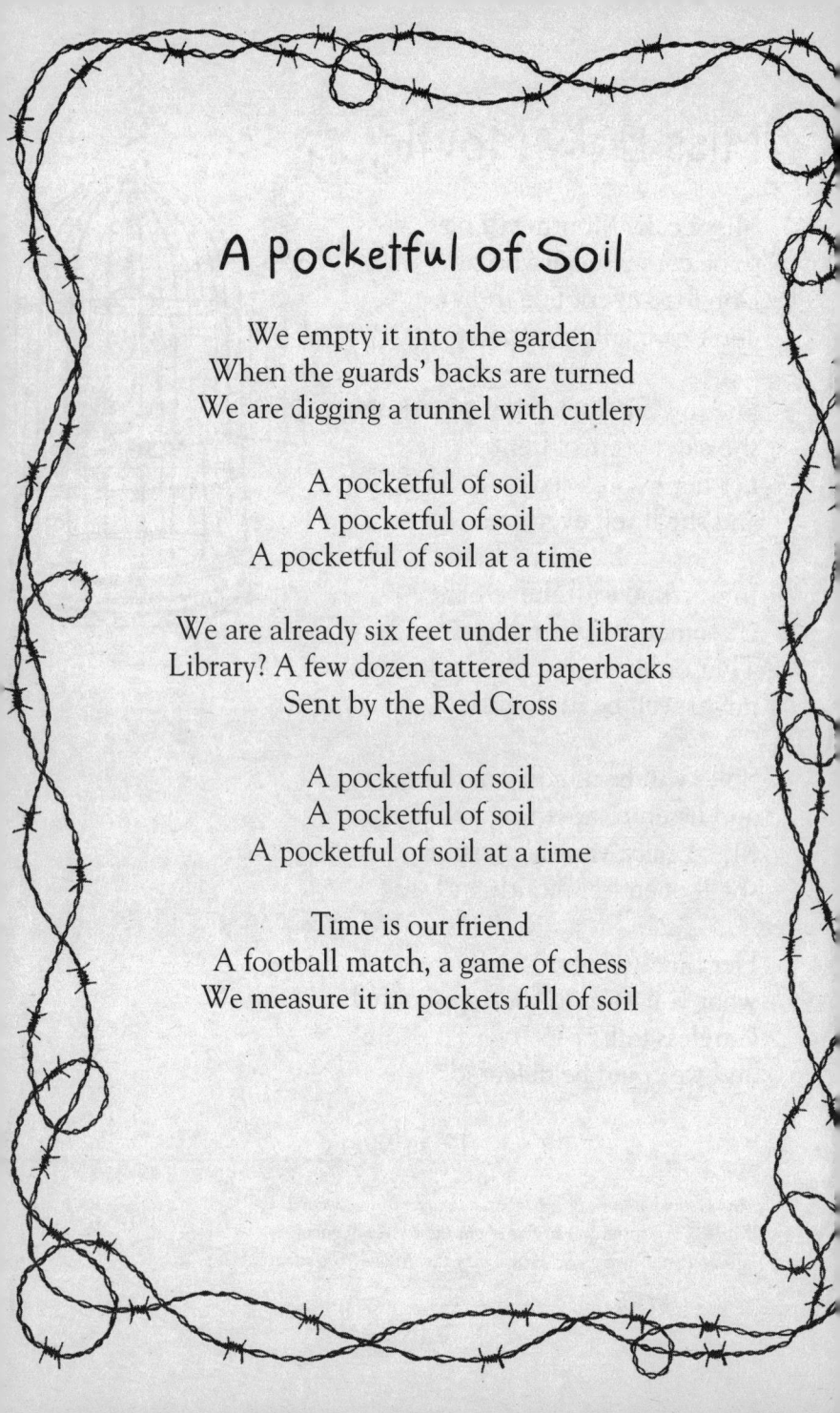

A Pocketful of Soil

We empty it into the garden
When the guards' backs are turned
We are digging a tunnel with cutlery

A pocketful of soil
A pocketful of soil
A pocketful of soil at a time

We are already six feet under the library
Library? A few dozen tattered paperbacks
Sent by the Red Cross

A pocketful of soil
A pocketful of soil
A pocketful of soil at a time

Time is our friend
A football match, a game of chess
We measure it in pockets full of soil

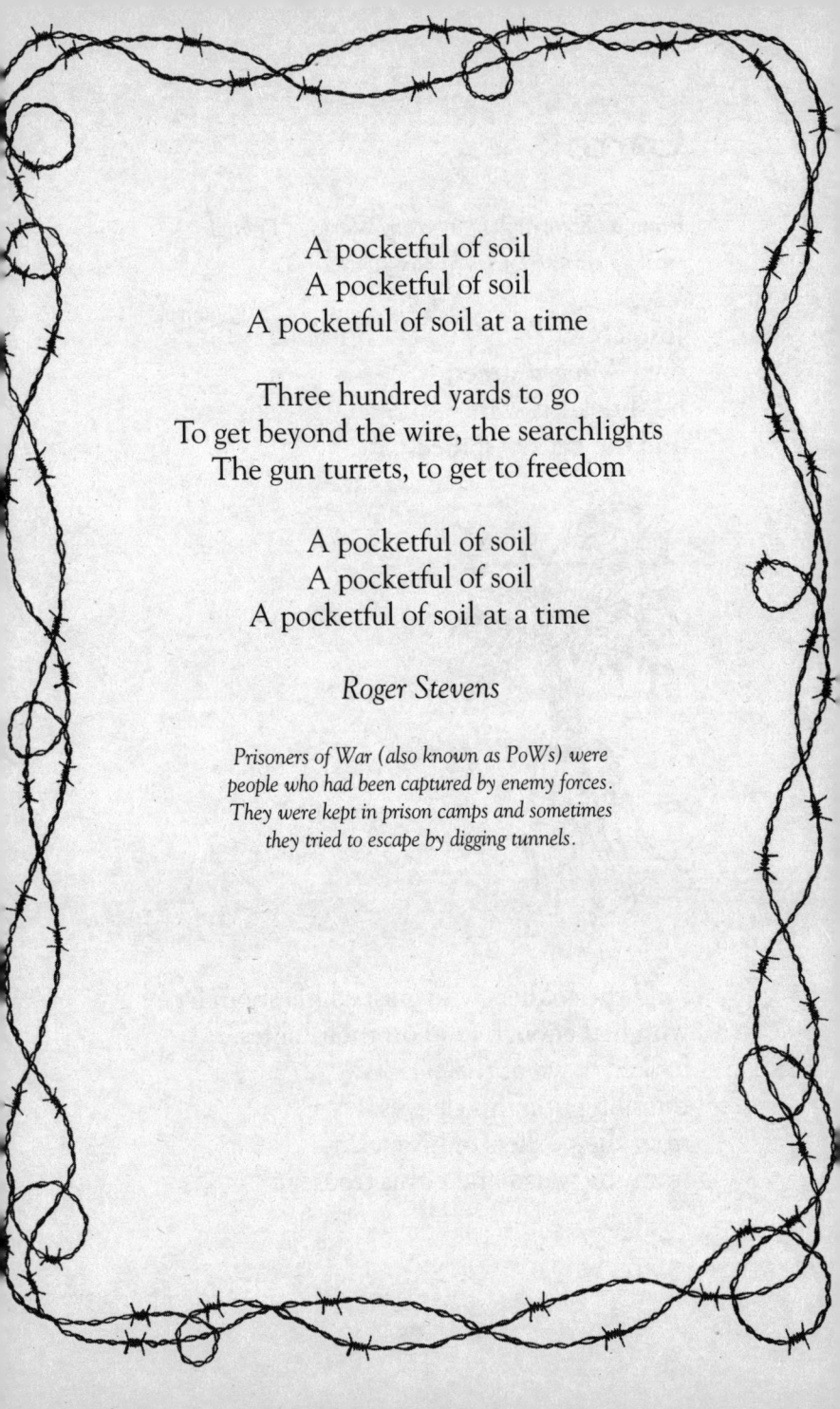

A pocketful of soil
A pocketful of soil
A pocketful of soil at a time

Three hundred yards to go
To get beyond the wire, the searchlights
The gun turrets, to get to freedom

A pocketful of soil
A pocketful of soil
A pocketful of soil at a time

Roger Stevens

*Prisoners of War (also known as PoWs) were
people who had been captured by enemy forces.
They were kept in prison camps and sometimes
they tried to escape by digging tunnels.*

Carrots

From a photograph of a boy in Warsaw, Poland,
stealing carrots for his family

Just a boy
on a Warsaw street,
he shook his shirt
and the carrots spilled out.

And the soldiers who grasped his shoulders,
who had enough food on their tables,
looked down at the carrots
tumbling from his sleeves,
from the pockets of his jacket,
from the waistband of his trousers.

And they photographed him,
the lad from the ghetto,
stealing carrots
so his family might eat.

And I could see,
in the twisted faces of the soldiers,
that he was about to receive
some terrible punishment.

And I thought about me,
when I was his age.
Would I have done
what he did?
Fought for food,
risked everything
for just carrots?

Brian Moses

*During the Second World War, many Jewish
families in Poland, Germany and Austria were
imprisoned in overcrowded ghettos before being
moved to concentration camps. There was little
food and so families would often have to beg or
steal to survive.*

Subterfuge

Fooled you!
We fooled you!
Those tanks weren't real
They were made of wood
We fooled you, yes
We fooled you good.

And the real tanks
Were in disguise
Didn't you know
Or realize
That the desert sun
Can play tricks
With your eyes?

Roger Stevens

During the Second World War, the military constructed whole units of fake tanks. Real tanks were also disguised using fabric to look like normal road vehicles.

VE Day

It was . . .
Lancaster bombers dropping red and green flares,
the peeling of bells, the whistle of tugs on the Thames.
It was . . .
Sailors climbing lamp posts, swinging by one arm,
policemen losing their helmets.
It was . . .
Bonfires lit, fireworks fizzling, dustbin lids clanging,
washing lines strung with red, white and blue clothes.
It was . . .
Paddling in the fountains in Trafalgar Square,
men's faces covered in lipstick kisses.
It was. . .
Grandad tearfully singing 'The White Cliffs of Dover'
and being pushed home from the celebrations
in a wheelbarrow.

Brian Moses

VE Day, which stands for Victory in Europe Day, was a public holiday held in Europe on the 8 May 1945 to celebrate the unconditional surrender of the German forces.

Shadows

Children playing in the street
In Hiroshima or Nagasaki
A mother's call
A clear blue sky
A bomb
(Just one – that's all)
Like a giant camera flash
And children's shadows
Burned upon a wall

Roger Stevens

In August 1945 the Americans dropped two atomic bombs on Japan, ending the Second World War. This is the only time that nuclear weapons have ever been used in warfare.

What Are We Fighting For?

'I object to violence because when it appears to do good, the good is only temporary; the evil it does is permanent'

Mahatma Gandhi

The War Factor

In comics, in the fifties, the Japanese would yell,
    'Banzai!'
And they'd blow the US trucks out of the way
But the Yanks are on a mission, they find the
    enemy's munitions
And KA-BOOM! Their army's now in disarray

In films, like *Spartacus*, *Ben-Hur* or *Gladiator*
We watch with glee the Romans' power play
Meanwhile Roman legions crush all the
    neighbouring regions
And woe betide the slaves who disobey

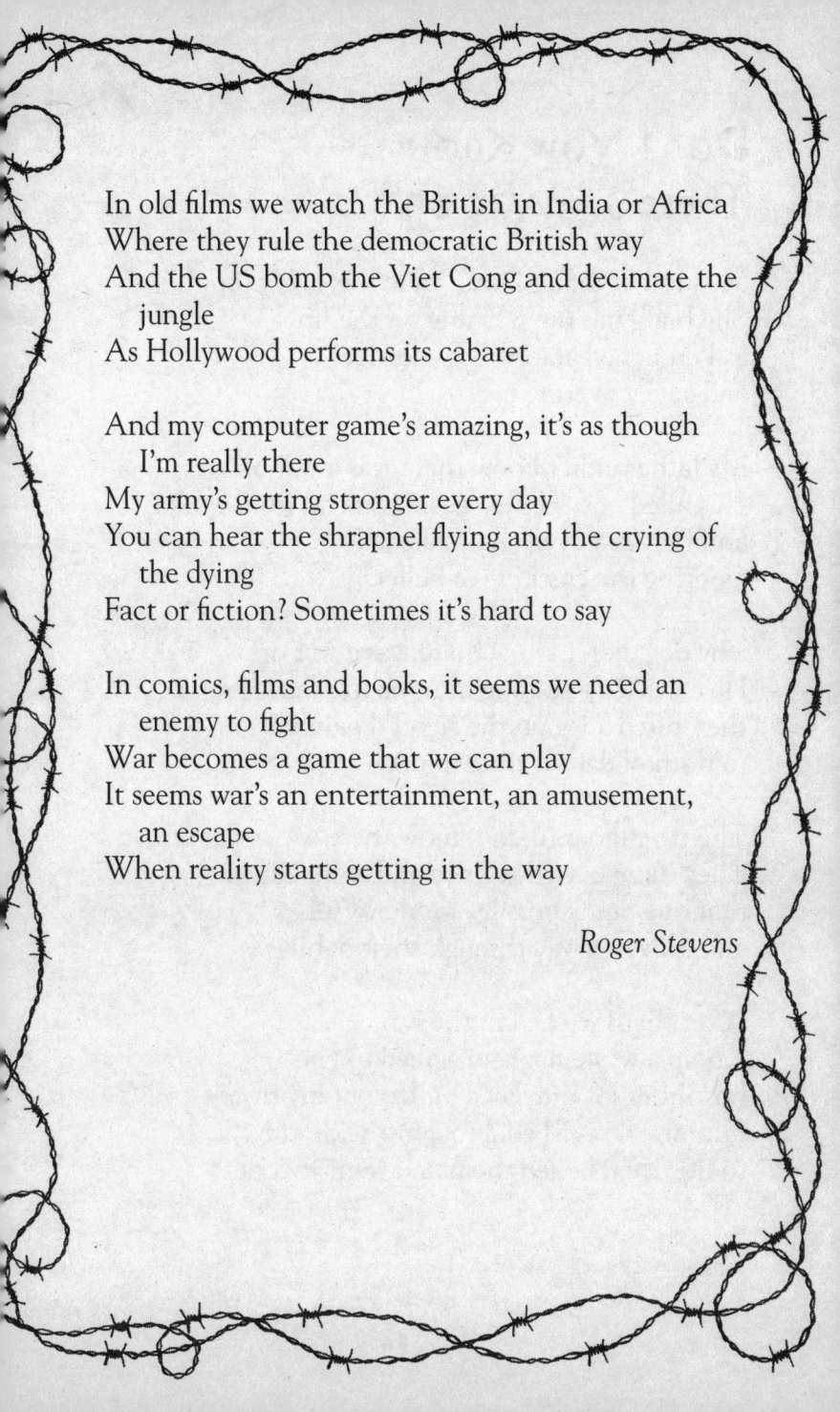

In old films we watch the British in India or Africa
Where they rule the democratic British way
And the US bomb the Viet Cong and decimate the
    jungle
As Hollywood performs its cabaret

And my computer game's amazing, it's as though
    I'm really there
My army's getting stronger every day
You can hear the shrapnel flying and the crying of
    the dying
Fact or fiction? Sometimes it's hard to say

In comics, films and books, it seems we need an
    enemy to fight
War becomes a game that we can play
It seems war's an entertainment, an amusement,
    an escape
When reality starts getting in the way

Roger Stevens

Don't You Know There's a War on?

My mother didn't know there was a war on.
She hung out the washing on the line
as I crouched among the cabbages
and gave covering fire.

My father didn't know there was a war on.
He called out, 'Hello,' as he came in from work
and I broke cover, shouted back,
ignoring the cracking of bullets.

The dog didn't know there was a war on.
He carried on sniffing in no-man's-land
then lifted a leg on the sign I'd painted
to warn of danger from mines.

The neighbours didn't know there was a war on.
They hung over the fence and complained
that one of my missiles went AWOL
and drove its way through their dahlias.

After that I packed in the war,
ran up a white flag and agreed to end
hostilities for the day. I pulled out my troops
from the flower-bed, brought the dead back
to life, then boxed them and went indoors.

There wasn't much for tea and when
I complained, Mum snapped, 'I thought you said
there's a war on, so how am I supposed
to bring supplies through a battle zone?'

Later I watched *The News* on TV.
It seemed there was a war on everywhere.
Perhaps I'll declare an outbreak of peace tomorrow.

Brian Moses

AWOL – absent without leave, gone missing

Missiles in Cuba

I was twelve years old
when Kennedy muscled up to Khrushchev over
    missiles in Cuba,
when Cold War bluff and counter-bluff took the world
    to the brink.
I learned a new word:
Armageddon.
'It could happen here,'
the papers proclaimed,
'It could happen now.'
I questioned my parents constantly, were we all about
    to die?
My father, grim-faced,
spoke only of the last lot,
of how they survived.
But the world had rolled on since then, more fuses,
    more firepower.
My eyes pleaded with him,
say it will be OK.
But he was frightened too,
I could tell.

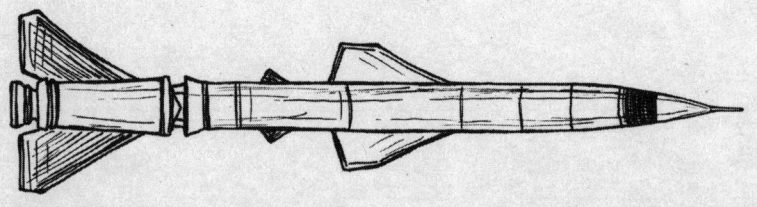

We tiptoed about the house,
it didn't seem right to play Elvis songs,
no 'Good Luck Charm' would stop this war,
I knew the score on that one.
And why should I worry about tests at school, we
    could all be blown to pieces
come the weekend.
My father said it was prayer that was needed,
but prayer wasn't doing any good.
And I remember that last-chance Sunday, all of us
    praying in church,
praying so hard it hurt,
then coming home to find
they'd backed away, stepped down from the abyss.

Out in the garden
I stood beneath the stars, breathed in,
breathed deep,
breathed a future.

Brian Moses

In 1962 the Russians started building nuclear-missile sites on Cuba, a communist island only ninety miles away from America. This was because the Americans had placed nuclear missiles in Turkey aimed at Moscow. People were scared it might be the start of a nuclear war.

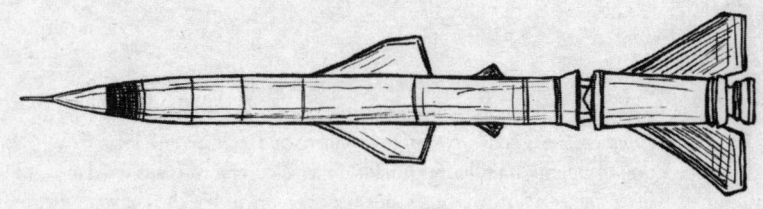

Vietnam Veterans' Memorial

Some people in the USA
Said better dead than red
And they thought that communists
Were underneath their beds

Now in Constitution Gardens
In a park in Washington
There's a memorial for veterans
Who died in Vietnam

Nearly sixty thousand soldiers
And every soldier's name
Better dead than red?
Ask the ghosts of those dead soldiers
If they still feel the same

Roger Stevens

*The colour red is associated with communism and can be found on
many flags of communist countries such as the Soviet Union and China.
Communism is both a type of government and an economic system (a
way of creating and sharing wealth) in which everyone is supposed to
share the wealth they create so no one has more or less than anyone else.*

Sniper

Mum gives Tarik a hug
Don't cross the square
It may be further via the church
But it's safe. You're not in open view.

And tell him, Belma sends her love
That might be worth an extra loaf or two
I know he has the flour still
And while you are there
Ask him, What news of Ivan?

Mum gives Tarik another hug
And whispers a short prayer
Go now, she says
And do not cross the square

Roger Stevens

Hide-and-Seek

You are hiding
In a confined space
It's cramped, uncomfortable
But no one is counting to a hundred
Coming! Ready or not!
Because it's not a game.
You may have to stay there
Silent and still
For an hour
Or a week
Or a year
And you are probably wondering
What you did wrong?
It's because you were born a Christian,
Or maybe a Muslim, or maybe a Jew
And an emperor, or a king
Or a dictator has decided
They don't agree with you

Roger Stevens

The War on Terror

To kill
Innocent
Men
And women and children
To tape a bomb
To your body
And walk into
A busy market
To fly
An aeroplane
Into a skyscraper
How strong
Your belief must be

And you must be free
To believe what you believe
But surely
Can you not see
Four thousand years
Of history
That says
Killing will achieve you nothing
And I mean nothing
For your cause
But a lot
Of suffering
And misery

Roger Stevens

Deadly Duo

Stealth bomber
You are like an owl
A ghostly shape
Swooping on your prey

Owl
You are a stealth bomber
The shrew looks up
Too late

Roger Stevens

Escalation

Billy took my apple
So I kicked Billy in the shins.

Billy's mate pushed me over
On the playground
And I dropped my lunch box

So my mate Dave
Punched Billy's mate
On the nose

Then all Billy's friends joined in
And so did mine
And everyone was fighting

And Jess was shouting
And screaming for me
And Tess told her to 'Shut up!'

And soon the girls were all at it too
And the dinner ladies came to sort it out
But Mrs Pickings said it was my fault

And Miss Brodie told her that she saw it all
And it wasn't and they started arguing
And Mrs Pickings hit her with her handbag

And the teachers had to come and sort it out
And it took a while
Because they were all arguing too

Luckily Mr Walton heard the rumpus
Came out of his office
And blew his whistle

And it all got sorted in the end
And me and Billy shook hands and said sorry
And he whispered to me

After school . . .
You're dead!

Roger Stevens

The Shouting Side

There's a war being waged
in our family,
Mum versus Dad,
in the middle there's me
and it's hard to decide
whose side I'm on
when they're both
on the shouting side.

Dad shouts at Mum,
Mum screams at Dad,
then they start on me
and it makes me mad,
I don't want to decide
whose side I'm on
when they're both
on the shouting side.

Can't they see,
can't they be quiet?
Why do they yell
like they're starting a riot?
They're acting this out
on a tiny stage,
there's no need to shout
or fly into a rage.

There's no need to take out
their feelings on me,
I'm trying to listen,
can't they see?
I'm standing here
with my ears wide open,
somebody please
be quietly spoken.

There's a war being waged
in our family,
Mum versus Dad,
in the middle there's me
and it's hard to decide
whose side I'm on
when they're both
on the shouting side.

Brian Moses

What Causes War?

Lust for power
Lust for land
How much soil
Does one man need?

Lust for gold
Lust for oil
There's no excuse
In one word – 'greed'

And religion too
Must share the blame
The sacred words
Ignored

Or changed to suit
The moneymakers
Building guns
And swords

As troubles breed
And wars increase
We need to know
What causes peace?

Roger Stevens

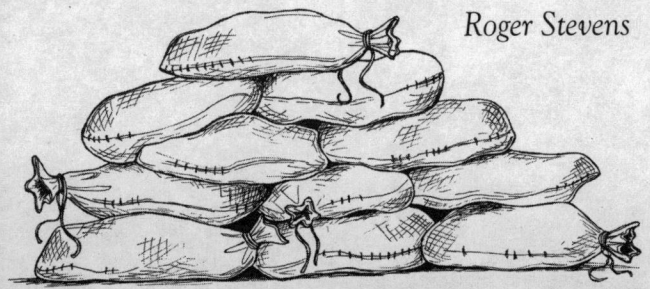

Spoils of War

Imagine, after humans have left the planet
And the new owners of Earth
Are digging about for signs of our past

There will probably be a TV programme
Intergalactic Time Team
Beamed across the universe

Aliens, delicately sifting soil
Looking for ancient artefacts
Trying to discover what our race was like

Excitement as the first items are found
An ancient sword, bullets, a rusted flamethrower
An unexploded mine

Roger Stevens

What Are We Fighting For?

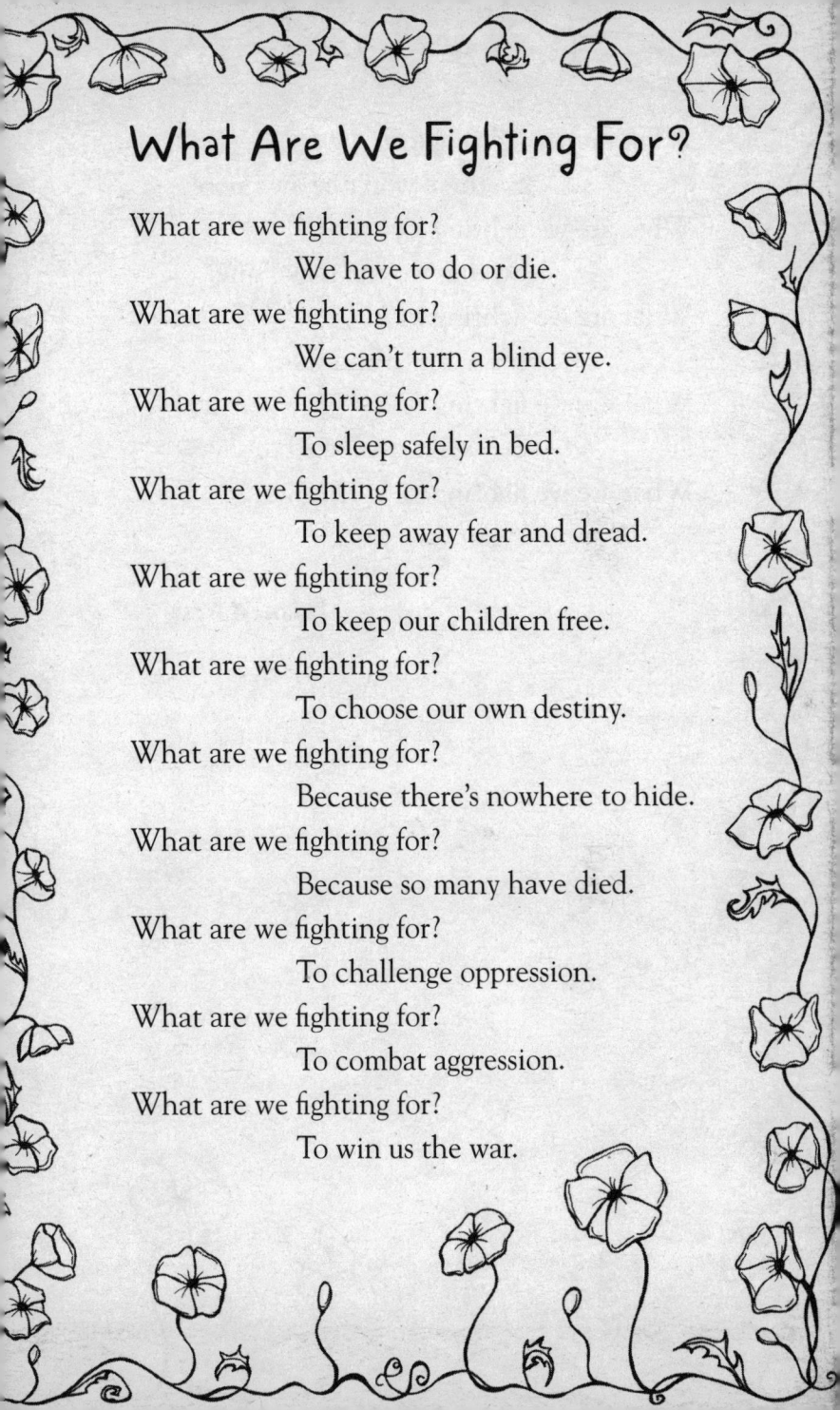

What are we fighting for?
>We have to do or die.

What are we fighting for?
>We can't turn a blind eye.

What are we fighting for?
>To sleep safely in bed.

What are we fighting for?
>To keep away fear and dread.

What are we fighting for?
>To keep our children free.

What are we fighting for?
>To choose our own destiny.

What are we fighting for?
>Because there's nowhere to hide.

What are we fighting for?
>Because so many have died.

What are we fighting for?
>To challenge oppression.

What are we fighting for?
>To combat aggression.

What are we fighting for?
>To win us the war.

What are we fighting for?
>So there won't be any more.

What are we fighting for?
>So that we can make sure.

What are we fighting for?
>It's a war to end war.

What are we fighting for?
>So we'll never need to say

What are we fighting for?
>Again.

Brian Moses

Index of First Lines

Epic Tales from

ADVENTURE TIME™

Queen of Rogues

by T. T. MacDangereuse

John

PSS!
Price Stern Sloan
An Imprint of Penguin Group (USA) LLC

PRICE STERN SLOAN
Published by the Penguin Group
Penguin Group (USA) LLC, 375 Hudson Street, New York, New York 10014, USA

USA I Canada I UK I Ireland I Australia I New Zealand I India I South Africa I China

penguin.com
A Penguin Random House Company

Published in 2014 by Price Stern Sloan, a division of Penguin Young Readers Group, 345 Hudson Street, New York, New York 10014. *PSS!* is a registered trademark of Penguin Group (USA) LLC. Printed in the USA.

Text written by Leigh Dragoon
Cover illustrated by Christopher Houghton

ISBN 978-0-8431-8035-0   10 9 8 7 6 5 4 3 2 1

Greetings, fans of epic adventure . . .

What you are holding in your hands is one of the most amazing novels in all of Ooo. These fantastical adventures by the master of awesome storytelling, T. T. MacDangereuse, are filled with tales of unimaginable heroism, perilous wonder, and unspeakable marvel. While some of these characters may seem familiar to you, keep in mind that nothing is what it seems when you enter the mind of T. T. MacDangereuse.

CHAPTER 1

Fionna's sweaty palms dampened her skirt as she lifted its hem and stepped onto the gangplank leading up to P. Gumball's massive yacht. She tried to focus on the ship's deck, just ten feet away, and on the laughter and music the wind carried to her ears. Just ten feet and she'd . . .

Be on a ship. Which was about to set sail. On the ocean.

Fear washed over her and she froze. She couldn't stop looking at the water, imagining the creatures lurking beneath its mercurial surface. Creatures with tentacles, spines, teeth as long as her arm, creatures that would be able to get her if she fell in. All it would take was a single misstep on that thin, slick plank . . . She shuddered. Despite her best intentions, Fionna's thalassophobia was getting the better of her.

"Glob, what's the problem?" Lumpy Space Prince whined. He tugged at her hand as he bobbed in the air beside her. "You wanted to go to this stupid party, so, like, let's get going."

Sweat stood out on Fionna's forehead. She licked her lips as a paper streamer floated past her. "I . . . I dunno. Maybe this wasn't such a good idea."

Lumpy Space Prince heaved a sigh that was overly dramatic, even for him, and folded his arms across his chubby chest. "This is so like you, Fionna. You drag me here all the way from Lumpy Space for this lumping party, and now you don't even want to go? Like, I totally should have expected this. You're the worst pretend girlfriend ever."

Fionna swallowed. She did want to go to the party. She'd been so excited when she and her roommate, Cake the Cat, had received their invitations just two days ago. The invites, pressed onto glittering sheets of ruby-red Candy cardstock, had been hand-delivered by a sharply attired Green Gumdrop. Fionna had been too shocked to say thank you as the Gumdrop tipped his bowler hat and took his leave.

"Actual invitations!" Cake had exclaimed. "Hon, that's incredible!" Her tail fuzzed with excitement. P. Gumball's parties were infamous. "And we each get to bring a plus one! I know who I'm asking—Lord Monochromicorn!"

Fionna's heart fluttered. P. Gumball was a famous recluse—everyone in Candy Kingdom had a fanciful story they'd heard from the son of an aunt of a brother of a sister of a father of a mouse, but who knew if any of those stories were true? According to the gossip she'd heard, Gumball was simultaneously ten feet tall, a half-orc, a ghost, and a werewolf. She'd heard that he had earned his wealth through mysterious, unsavory means involving demons and the Nightosphere; by falling into a sinkhole and discovering an enormous cache of diamonds; by keeping a herd of captive rainicorns who wept tears of pure gold; through an inheritance left to him by a kindly great-great-great-grandfather who had died of natural causes at the ripe old age of six hundred and five.

Fionna was no fool—she knew most everything was probably nonsense, but that only heightened her curiosity. And now she'd finally been given a chance to attend one of his parties, to meet the mysterious millionaire himself. She wasn't about to let a fear of the ocean get in the way of that.

Or so she'd told herself.

The wind picked up, luffing the yacht's sails, rocking the gangplank beneath Fionna's feet. Her stomach quivered. She swallowed hard and, struggling to calm herself, focused on the letters painted in gold on the ship's hull: *The Banoffee*. Glob, what kind of a name was that?

"Fionna! What the lump? Like, come on!"

Lumpy Space Prince was moments away from sinking into a good long pout, she realized. She struggled to hide her annoyance. He hadn't wanted to go, and she hadn't wanted to invite him, but everyone else had already paired up. She'd been determined not to be the only person without a plus one.

"A-all right." Lumpy Space Prince was right. They were already late. Cake had left hours ago, astride Lord Monochromicorn's rippling back. Taking a deep breath, she closed her eyes, dashed up the gangplank, and leaped onto the deck.

There. She breathed a sigh of relief. That was better.

"Like, finally. Well, we're here. What do you want to do now?"

On deck, the music was much, much louder. She could barely hear Lumpy Space Prince's complaints. As she took a look around, her jaw dropped. The entire deck was crowded with a dizzying array of guests. They milled about, talking, dancing, playing games. She caught sight of a huge buffet table loaded with cakes, pies, and pastries to her left. To her right, a group of golems and beetles were holding a painting competition involving eggs and large jars of mustard.

"This is the most amazing party I've ever been to," Fionna said, grinning.

Lumpy Space Prince scowled. "I've been to better."

"So where is he?" Fionna craned her neck. "Where's P. Gumball?"

Lumpy Space Prince shrugged. "Like, how am I supposed to know? I want some cake. I'll see you around."

"Wait—" Too late. Lumpy Space Prince was

already floating away from her. "Well, fine," Fionna muttered. She didn't need him around █████████ n. Scanning the deck, she spotted Cak ███████████ 'd Monochromicorn dancing.

Fionna waited until there was a lul██████ and waved her hand frantically over her ████

Cake waved back, smiled, and stre████ in an arch over the crowd. "Here, lemr███ g lift," she said, holding out her paws. Fi█████ on and bit back a yelp as she was wh████ away, then set down gently beside her ██████

"I was starting to get worried abc████ said, smoothing wrinkles from Fionnc████ are you so late?"

Fionna rolled her eyes. "I came with Lumpy Space Prince."

Cake snorted. "Enough said."

Lord Monochromicorn stamped his left hoof, five slow taps, followed by three quick ones. Fionna glanced at Cake, waiting for her to translate. "He says you're here now, so you may as well start having a good time."

Fionna grinned. The wind had died, and the ship was almost motionless. The sky was cloudless and glassy with stars. It was easy to forget they were on the water. She spread her arms and pirouetted on the deck. Cake formed her body into a ring and spun around Lord Monochromicorn's long neck.

"Look!" Cake shouted. "I'm a Hula-Hoop!"

Gasping with laughter, Fionna whirled to a stop. Dizzy, she stumbled back a step and bumped into a pink-haired young man carrying a silver tray. The young man fumbled and nearly dropped the tray.

"Oh!" Fionna said. "Excuse me." He must have been the caterer—his tray was piled with multicolored pastries.

"Not a problem, I've got it." He smiled and held the tray of deliciousness out toward her. "Please, try one. They're fresh out of the oven."

Fionna's eyes widened. They all looked amazing and smelled great, like lilacs and strawberries. She hesitated, then selected a lime-green puff pastry that was absolutely dripping with glaze.

"How is it?" Cake asked as Fionna popped the treat into her mouth. A delicate mixture of fruit flavors exploded across her tongue.

"Amazing!" she said.

The caterer inclined his head. "Thanks so much." His eyes were a deep, glittering purple. Fionna felt her cheeks flush and she nervously patted at her hair. Too late, she remembered the glaze coating her fingers.

"Here, lemme try one," Cake said. She shoveled a fistful of pastries into her mouth. "Glob! These are so good!"

Grateful for the distraction, Fionna yanked her hand away from her hair and wiped her fingers on the back of her gown.

"You're really talented," Cake was saying. "You're definitely gonna have to cater my next party."

Fionna rubbed her arms. The night had grown cold. Her breath fogged in the air. A handful of white flecks fluttered past her face. Confetti?

No, she realized, not confetti. Snow. "What the—"

A huge bolt of lightning stuttered across the sky, followed almost immediately by a peal of thunder so loud Fionna clapped her hands over her ears. The music jangled to a halt and, in the sudden silence, a swirling cloud of freezing-cold air billowed across the center of the deck. People screamed and staggered clear as the vapor thinned, revealing a tall, stately figure clad in an elaborate royal-blue gown.

"The Ice Queen!" Fionna whispered.

Chapter 2

"Where is he?" the Ice Queen shouted at the terrified partygoers. "Where's Gumball? Don't force me to turn everyone into popsipeople!"

The caterer stepped past Fionna and cleared his throat. "I'm P. Gumball," he said.

A collective gasp filled the air. The caterer? Fionna's jaw nearly hit the ground. The *caterer* was the famous, mysterious, inscrutable P. Gumball? She couldn't believe it. Gumball held the tray of desserts out toward the Ice Queen. "Pastry?"

"No, I don't want any flipping pastries!" Her eyes flashed as she slapped the tray out of his hands. "I've got a major bone to pick with you. It's bad enough you never invite me to any of your swank hootenannies, but this is just unacceptable!" She jabbed a long, pointy fingernail at Fionna. "You won't invite me, but you'll invite a stinky little tomboy nobody like this . . . this Finnona?"

"Hey!" Fionna shouted. "First off, you got no business knocking things around like that. And secondly, it's Fionna!"

"See, I can't even remember her name!" Coils of wrathful snow churned around the Ice Queen's feet. "That's how much of a nobody she is!"

"Ice Queen, please, calm yourself," Gumball said. "I don't invite you to my parties because I don't like you. You know. As a person."

"Dude, too harsh," Cake said in a stunned voice. Fionna had to agree. She'd had just enough run-ins with the powerful sorceress, saving various princes from being kidnapped by her, to know such frankness was a terrible idea. Indeed, the Ice Queen's face had gone even whiter, her eyes bulged nearly out of her skull, and her entire body shook with rage. Frost crept along and snow blanketed the deck. The Candy guests shrank away from the Ice Queen, huddling against the railings and under the buffet table.

Fionna had to give Gumball credit. In the face of the queen's rapidly escalating anger, he stood firm, his arms crossed over his chest, his expression one of utter indifference.

"This is unacceptable!" A horrible, grating voice Fionna recognized as belonging to Lemongrab rang out over the deck. "So rude! So rude!" She began to scream, an ear-bleedingly awful noise.

"That's enough out of you!" the Ice Queen cried. A barrage of snow magic erupted from her hands and encased Lemongrab, head to toe, in three feet of ice.

"See?" Gumball's voice was frostily calm. "This is exactly why you're not invited to my shwings."

"That's it!" the Ice Queen screamed. "We are moving this party back to my Ice Fortress, where it's going to be about a million times better, and everyone is going to have a good time, whether they like it or not!"

"Um, I don't mean to be rude, but my dad really wants me home." Lumpy Space Prince floated tentatively forward. "Like, four hours ago. So, like . . . I'm just gonna leave."

"You're not going anywhere!" The Ice Queen's hands glowed with a foreboding blue light.

"Okay, this has gone on just slightly too long enough." Fionna shoved herself forward, getting all up in the Ice Queen's face. "I don't need my sword to kick your icy butt all the way back to your crummy ice castle."

The queen sneered down at her. "Strong words for someone who brought Lumpy Space Prince as her plus one."

With a cry, Fionna lunged at the queen, her fist poised to land a beautiful punch across the queen's kisser. Then her left foot came down, slipped out from under her, and too late she realized the deck around the queen was coated with ice. Her back slammed into the deck, knocking the air out of her lungs.

"Look at this!" The Ice Queen shook a fist at Gumball. "Her legs don't even work right!"

Snarling, Fionna lurched to her feet. "Cake, battle-club mode!" In a flash Cake had shape-changed into a giant club crowned with spikes. Fionna gripped the handle and dropped into a fighting stance.

The queen held her hand out behind her, fingers splayed, and gestured toward the knot of terrified partygoers. "You take one step toward me, and I'll freeze them all." The queen's lips quirked into a smile. "Stalemate, tomboy."

Fionna scowled. "I can stay like this all night."

"Well, I can't," Lumpy Space Prince said

peevishly. "I seriously have to be home soon."

"Oh my glob, Lumpy Space Prince, shut up!" Cake snapped.

"The boy's right," the Ice Queen said. "I really don't feel like breaking any nails over you. Listen, Gumball, why don't we make things interesting? How about we see how fast your little boat can go? I propose a race."

Gumball nodded stiffly. "I accept."

Fionna felt all the blood drain from her face. A boat race. On the ocean? It was bad enough being in a ship that was tied to a nice safe dock. But to be out, over miles and miles of nothingness filled with unspeakable monsters?

"Then we're on!" the Ice Queen cackled. "Whoever makes it to the Island Guy first is the winner." She swooped into the air and blasted the ocean with her magic. The water roiled, waves slapping against the side of Gumball's ship. Fionna cried out, lost her grip on Cake, and dropped into a crouch.

"Hold steady, girl!" Cake braced herself against Fionna, propping them both up.

With a sound like icebergs grinding against one another, a massive shape rose out of the ocean. Dripping water, it solidified into a towering ship. Masts made from sheets of frost luffed in the wind. The figurehead on the prow formed into a likeness of the Ice Queen herself.

The Ice Queen nodded in satisfaction and glanced back at Gumball. "I'm sure you'll understand if I'm not quite sure how much I can trust you, so I'm going to take a little collateral." With a sweep of her arm, the Ice Queen whisked all the terrified partygoers over the side of the ship—everyone except Fionna, Cake, and Gumball—and dumped them on her boat's deck. "All right," she said. "If you get there before me, you can have all your little friends back. But if I get there first, you have to marry me. And you're going to have to pretend you like it!"

Laughing, the Ice Queen swooped onto her ship's forecastle. She waved her arms and a thick mantle of murky clouds fanned out across the sky. The frost-sails strained against the spars, and the Ice Queen's ship scuttled away into the distance. The rising storm quickly drowned out the frantic keening of her hostages.

Gumball's eyes shone with excitement as he sprinted across the deck and began unfastening the mooring ropes. "I need one of you guys to take the helm," he called. "Just until we're out of port."

"Come on." Cake tugged at Fionna's arm. "We gotta get my main squoosh back!"

"A-all right." Fionna swallowed, pushing her fear down deep into the pit of her food-pouch. She scrambled to her feet. "Where's the helm?"

"This way." Cake shot up a flight of stairs leading up to another deck. Fionna stumbled after her.

"Okay, turn the wheel hard to the right," Gumball shouted as they positioned themselves behind the heavy oak steering wheel.

"Your right or our right?" Cake asked.

"Um . . . your right."

"Here we go." Fionna grabbed the top of the wheel and jerked it down hard. The ship lurched toward the dock.

"No, my right, my right!"

"What the glob!" Cake's tail had puffed out to three times its normal size. She and Fionna spun the wheel frantically. The ship swung back the other way and slipped away from the dock.

"I thought you knew how to sail this thing," Cake snapped as Gumball clambered up the stairs.

"I know a great deal about sailing and ship masonry." Gumball wiped sweat from his forehead and grinned. "It's just that some of my knowledge is a bit . . . academic."

"So, what, you read some book about it?" Fionna asked.

"Books. Plural. And I assure you, they were very thorough books."

Fionna pushed her hair out of her eyes and stared at Gumball in bewilderment. Just what had she and Cake gotten themselves into?

"This yacht was built according to my own plans. I've been dying to put her through her paces." Gumball rubbed his chin. "Though we don't seem to be going as fast as my research indicated. Oh! The sails. I need to trim them. Hold her steady, I'll be right back."

"I think we're in trouble here, Cake," Fionna said as Gumball leaped down the stairs and ran to the mainmast.

Cake scowled. "Don't I know it."

Whatever Gumball did worked. By the time he rejoined them at the helm, the ship had picked up speed. Fionna squinted at the horizon and could just make out the masts of the Ice Queen's vessel. A tear slipped down Cake's cheek, and Fionna put a comforting arm around her friend's shoulders. "Don't worry," she said. "We'll catch up with them. You'll be back with Lord Monochromicorn in no time."

"Yeah." Cake swiped at her eyes. "And then I'm gonna make that woman sorry she ever decided to mess with us."

CHAPTER 3

After half an hour, it began to snow, and it thickened as Gumball's yacht closed the gap between them and the Ice Queen's ship. Small icebergs dotted the water.

"I bet she's trying to slow us down," Cake muttered.

"At least the wind's holding steady," Gumball said. "The current here is pushing against us. We should all keep a sharp eye on these icebergs. We don't want to hit any of them."

Fionna opened her mouth to interject a comment of her own. Instead, she threw up all over her shoes.

"Girl, why didn't you say you were feeling sick?"

Cake chided. "That's just gross."

"I . . . I . . ." She couldn't say anything more. She felt sweaty and even more nauseous than she had before she'd thrown up. She shivered and rubbed her bare arms. Of all the days to be stuck wearing a sleeveless gown. Cake hopped onto Fionna's back and quickly formed herself into a hoodie.

"Fionna, you should have told me." Gumball dug into his jacket pocket and pulled out a floppy gold band. "Put this around your wrist. It'll help, I promise."

Fionna took the band. It was translucent, and slightly warm, with the texture and flexibility of a fresh gummy worm. When she slipped it over her hand, it shrank. As it squeezed her wrist, its color flashed from gold to green. Immediately, she felt better. The nausea and dizziness subsided. "Wow, thanks, Gumball. What is this thing?"

"Anti-seasickness leech." Gumball grinned. "I invented it. And please, call me PG."

A sudden blast of wind howled through the rigging, and the ship lurched forward with enough force to knock all of them off their feet.

"Now we're cooking with fire!" Cake jumped up and grabbed the wheel. Gumball's yacht cut cleanly through the waves. In moments they'd drawn close enough to the queen's vessel for Fionna to make out the features of the captive party guests. The queen had created a giant ice cage on the center of the main deck, and packed every single one of them inside. Lord Monochromicorn's noble head jutted out of the top.

"I'm coming, baby!" Cake shouted as Lord Monochromicorn neighed.

"We are so going to win. I knew this ship was awesome," Gumball said. "Turn a bit to the left. We want a little more space between us when we pass her."

"Which left?" Cake shrieked.

"Starboard! Starboard!"

"There aren't any Star People on board!" Cake

and Fionna shouted in unison.

"Pretend there's one that way!" Gumball pointed. Cake swore as she jerked the wheel. They slipped alongside the Ice Queen's ship.

Fionna scanned the deck. "Where's the Ice Queen? I don't see her."

"There she is." Gumball pointed up at the crow's nest.

Just as they were about to pull ahead of the ice ship, the queen waved her arm, and a bolt of magic shot from her hand toward them. The yacht lurched in the water and canted sharply to the left.

Fionna gasped. "What did she do?"

Gumball ran to the back of the ship and peered over the railing. "She iced the rudder! We can't steer."

Cake pounded the wheel, spitting with rage. "That's cheating!"

The Ice Queen bared her pointy teeth in a wide grin and waved at them. "It's only cheating if it's someone else doing it to me!" she called as her ship floated away from them again.

"Can you move the rudder at all?" Gumball asked. Both Cake and Fionna threw themselves against it. It didn't budge.

Fionna eyed the increasingly large icebergs floating past them. "This is bad."

"That's such an understatement! We're floating through an ice field and we can't steer," Cake said. "Sister, we've gone straight past bad and into catastrophic!"

As if their worst fears had suddenly materialized, a huge iceberg swept straight toward them.

"Maybe I can block it." Cake licked her lips and stared at the oncoming berg.

Fionna grabbed her friend's arm. "Don't you even try. It's too big—you'll be crushed. The wind's still strong—can you glide us out of here?"

"Not the both of you, not at the same time."

"What's the alternative?"

"Quick," Gumball said. "The lifeboats. We're out of options."

Fionna and Cake exchanged glances and ran after Gumball as he tore down the deck. Working together, they yanked the canvas cover off one of the tiny crafts. Fionna was so terrified she couldn't even begin to allow herself to think. Just then they heard a thunderous crunch. A massive shudder tore through the whole ship.

"Hurry, push it over!" Gumball shouted.

"I got a better idea." Cake's arms shot out like rubbery serpents and wrapped themselves five or six times around the lifeboat. "Stand back!" She hefted it over the side of the boat and set it gently in the water. "Okay, now you guys." Keeping one hand on the rocking craft to hold it steady, she twined her other arm first around Fionna, then Gumball, lowering them into the boat before finally hopping down herself. Not a moment too soon—the yacht was listing in the water, slowly keeling over onto its side. It slipped beneath the waves, sucked down into the steel-gray depths.

"Well, poop." Gumball heaved a sigh as he stared forlornly at the handful of fat bubbles that were the only sign his ship had ever existed. "On her maiden voyage, no less." A particularly large wave rolled beneath the lifeboat, drenching them with spray, and Gumball stumbled against the side of the boat. Cake and Fionna shouted and grabbed at his shoulders as he nearly tumbled out into the frigid water.

"Be careful!" Fionna shoved him down into the bottom of the boat and collapsed on one of the plain wooden benches, head in her hands.

"It's all right," Gumball said. "I've read a ton of books about swimming as well."

"In freezing water?" Cake snorted.

Fionna's pulse pounded through her skull. She pressed her fists against her temples. The ocean. Miles and miles of water. Her head swam with fear. "So what do we do now?" she managed. "It's getting dark."

Gumball lurched to his feet. "I'll put the oars in the oarlocks and we can—"

"Sit down!" Fionna and Cake shouted. Gumball dropped back into the bottom of the boat with a hurt look on his face.

"You are testing my patience," Cake snapped. "Just stay there."

"Where are the oars?" Fionna asked. Gumball pointed. They were lashed against the sides of the craft, secured beneath the middle bench. Fionna and Cake unfastened them and dropped them into the oarlocks. The wind stiffened and Fionna's entire body broke out in goosebumps.

"Cake, I'm freezing," Fionna said. The air was so cold it stung her throat when she breathed. Cake slipped back around Fionna's torso, turning into a parka.

"How about you?" Cake asked, glancing at Gumball. "You doing okay?"

"Don't worry about me. My motto's 'always be prepared.'" Gumball reached into his suit jacket and pulled out a small pink rectangle. He unfolded it and shook it out with a snap, revealing a cloak, which he wrapped around his shoulders. "Thermal blanket. My own invention. Lightweight and super-snuggly."

Fionna cupped her hands and blew on them, then grabbed the oars. "We better get going."

Cake stretched her neck out past Fionna's head and glanced down at the water. "The current's pushing us in the wrong direction. It's going to be murder to row against."

Fionna frowned. "If we go with the current, and make it back to port, can we get another ship?"

"If we do that, we'll never be able to catch up with the Ice Queen, much less have a hope of reaching the Island Guy ahead of her," Gumball said. "Anyway, at this point we're probably much closer to the Island Guy than to port."

Fionna groaned.

"I could make myself into a sail," Cake said, "And we could tack against it."

Fionna glanced at Gumball. "I don't suppose you've got another blanket in there?"

"I don't, but there's enough room for us both to fit in this one." Gumball's irises glistened and wobbled handsomely. "It's snuggly."

"Hey, hey, there'll be none of that," Cake said. "I can do two things at once." She held up one of her skinny arms and opened her hand. As Fionna and Gumball watched, her hand expanded until it was the size of a large bedspread. It filled with wind and they scuttled forward.

"Mathematical!" Grinning, Fionna shipped the oars. They were still in the race and, with luck, maybe they could still win.

CHAPTER 4

Fionna peered over the side of the lifeboat, her hands clamped in a death grip on the smooth wood. Things were moving in the water beneath them. Large things. Things that left a glowing trail behind their sleek bodies in the water.

Things with teeth. Lots of sharp teeth.

She shuddered.

"I keep telling you, stop looking," Cake said, using her free, non-sail hand to grab Fionna's head and drag her back into a sitting position on the bench.

"I can't help it. I can't stop thinking about what might be down there."

"You better start helping it. You get yourself so worked up, it's making me nervous."

"Don't worry, Fionna," Gumball said. He craned his head over the side of the boat and stared down into the water. "I'm pretty sure that's just a school of pelagic, shark-toothed, ten-tentacled snappers. But considering how slow they're moving, and that reddish tint in the water, I think it's safe to say they've fed recently. They probably won't mess with us. Anyhoo, this time of year, in these waters, I'm thinking the only thing we have to worry about are flying jellyfish. Those can be nasty. I read one story where this guy got caught in a whole swarm of them, and he ended up so horribly scarred, his own family couldn't recognize him."

"Gumball," Cake said. "Stop. Helping."

Fionna clenched her jaw to keep her teeth from chattering and swallowed around a huge lump in her throat. "Maybe we could hop off this boat and camp out on one of those nice big icebergs for a little bit," she said. "Just for a little while. They seem so much more . . . stable."

"That's because for icebergs like this, 90 percent of their mass is below the surface of the water," Gumball piped up.

"Will you give it a rest?" Cake made an exasperated sound. "It's going to be dark soon. I'm going to glide up and see if I can spot any landmarks."

"Yeah!" Fionna said. "Landmarks. I love that idea. Love it. Landmarks are on land! Hurry and look. Gumball, let me under that blanket until she gets back."

Cake unwrapped herself and spread her body out into a giant kite while Fionna ducked under the blanket with Gumball. "Here, Fionna." Cake threw her right foot to Fionna, and Fionna caught it reflexively. It had shape-changed into a spool. "Hold on tight! And no funny business," Cake said. Her leg thinned and stretched into a slim rope, and with a jerk she disappeared as the wind sucked her up into the sky.

Gumball coughed and cleared his throat, and Fionna was suddenly very aware of how close they were sitting. The boat felt very, very small. She felt herself flush and stifled a groan. She looked like a gallon of pulped tomatoes when she blushed, all patchy and spotty.

"I hope we're almost there," she said quickly.

"Hmmm . . . Fionna, I have something to tell you." Gumball's voice was low, mesmerizing.

Fionna couldn't stop herself—she turned and met his luminous eyes. "Yeah?" Her voice sounded breathy and strange, not like her voice at all.

"Fionna. . . ." Gumball met her gaze. "Your breath . . . is terrible. Probably from all that puking earlier. Could you maybe, I dunno, gargle with some seawater? If you don't mind."

Fionna stared at Gumball as every thought in

her head jammed in her think-pipe. Her eyes felt like they were going to pop out of her skull. She fought down an urge to smack Gumball. Moving jerkily, she leaned far enough over the side of the boat to cup a hand of icy-cold water but even being that close to the water was too much for her. She couldn't do it. She pretended to scoop up a handful of water and tip it into her mouth. She swished the air in her mouth and "spit" into the water. When she sat back up, she clenched her knees with her fists and stared straight ahead, waiting for her face to cool.

"So, PG," she said when she felt calm enough. "What's the deal with the alterego? Why pretend to be the caterer at your own parties? If you don't want to be there, why throw them in the first place?" She stole a glance out of the corner of her eye and was pleased to see Gumball's cheeks redden a bit.

"Well, it's mostly that I love baking," he said. "I started throwing intimate dinner parties so I could show off my mad skills. But I want to keep pushing myself to improve, and once people knew who I was, all they did was kiss my butt-meats. I couldn't get an honest opinion out of anybody."

"So you decided to hide your identity?"

Gumball shrugged. "What better way to hide than in plain sight? The happiest day of my life was when Elbow Prince spit out a petit four I'd dusted with stink-worms and said it was the worst thing he'd ever eaten. That's when I knew I'd finally be able to reach the heights I aspired to."

Despite herself, Fionna smiled. "I can respect that," she said.

"Heads up!" Cake's voice rang out moments before she swooped down over the boat, missing Fionna's head by inches.

"Well?" Fionna shot to her feet, setting the boat rocking dangerously. "Are we close?"

"Not even," Cake said, turning herself back into

Fionna's parka. "I can't see nothing. Or, I guess I mean, all I can see is nothing. Oh, excuse me, I did see one thing. Big fog bank, heading straight toward us. So now we can be even more cold and wet. It'll be a great way to spend the night."

"Spend the night? Out here?" Fionna gasped.

"Keep it together, girl."

"It'll be all right," Gumball said. "Why, if we're lucky, we may be able to see a school of bioluminescing eyeball stingers. Don't worry, the name is a misnomer. They don't sting your eyes, they lay eggs on them, and then the eggs hatch and the larvae drill into your eyeballs and eat your retinas. But that would only happen if you stuck your face in the water while they pass by. Though I suppose if the wind kicks up enough spray—"

"GUMBALL!" Cake slapped her hand across the young man's mouth. "You need to quit it with the science lessons."

Gumball looked hurt and lapsed into what Fionna was pretty sure was a funk.

Just as Cake had predicted, as the sun dipped below the horizon, a massive fog bank surrounded them. Condensation dripped from everything, and Fionna tucked her hands inside her Cake-shirt. The thick fog deadened sound, making it difficult to hear someone even a few feet away.

"Well, this sucks," Cake said.

Fionna shivered and crossed her arms over her chest. "You can say that again."

"Hey, what's that?" Cake pointed at a spot just behind them.

Fionna turned and saw a huge shadow slip through the fog. Moments later, a perfectly ginormous ship appeared, looming above them. Fionna craned her head back on her neck. *Marshall Lee* was emblazoned down the entire side of the ship in huge, gold-trimmed block letters. The sails were colored dark black, and polished wooden skulls decorated the railings. The figurehead was a weird, two-headed thing that was like nothing Fionna had ever seen.

"Hey!" Fionna leaped to her feet and waved her arms above her head.

"Here, try this." Gumball pulled a star-shaped magenta candy from inside his jacket's breast pocket and handed it to her.

"Throw me! Throw me!" the star cried in a joyous, high-pitched voice.

"Let's sling it, Cake!" Fionna dropped the star into Cake's waiting hand. Fionna whirled Cake's flexible arm in a loop, building up momentum. The star shrieked with excitement.

"Faster! Faster!"

"Now, Cake!" Fionna released Cake's arm and they threw the star toward the *Marshall Lee* as hard as they could. Fionna held her breath as she watched the star reach the apex of its arc. What was going to—

The star exploded into a blindingly white shower of sparks that suffused the fog with light.

"Oh my goodness gracious!" Cake ducked her head down behind Fionna's back.

"Wheeeeee!" the sparks exclaimed as the wind swept them away.

Though the wind remained steady, and the ship's sails full, it slowly came to a stop beside their tiny lifeboat. "It worked," Fionna whispered.

"Yeah, but now what?" Cake muttered.

A figure, backlit by the last fading fingers of daylight, leaned out over the side of the *Marshall Lee*. Though the person's face was cast in deep shadow, their eyes glowed with a dull reddish light. Fionna shuddered as the strange, unearthly eyes met her own. Then the person ducked back behind the railing.

"Wow," Gumball said. "That guy's eyes are freaky. Maybe this isn't such a good idea."

"Versus what?" Cake snapped, unwrapping

herself from Fionna and staring at Gumball with her hands on her hips. "Rowing in circles all night waiting to get our retinas eaten?"

"Shush!" Fionna hissed. A rope ladder slipped down the *Marshall Lee*'s hull. Her own personal misgivings aside, Fionna was willing to trade a lung for anything that would get her out of the tiny lifeboat. She snagged the bottom rung of the rope ladder with one of the oars. Fionna tossed her slippers into the bottom of the lifeboat and wedged her foot into the bottom rung, gripping the coarse hemp with her toes. "Hold this steady and wait here," she told the others. "I'll check it out." Sucking in a deep breath, she began to climb.

CHAPTER 5

Rough rope fibers bit into Fionna's fingers and toes as she climbed. The sun had slipped down below the horizon, and the thickening twilight made the climbing even more difficult. Fat pink sponges, each roughly the size of her fist, clung like barnacles to the hull. As the boat rolled with the waves, the ladder swung at least five or six feet back and forth. She'd almost reached the top when a particularly rough wave rocked the ship. The ladder swung Fionna toward the hull. She gasped, slapped her hand against the hull, and braced herself. Her hand came down right on top of a sponge, which squished unpleasantly. Foul-smelling liquid oozed between her fingers. Gritting her teeth, Fionna wiped her hand on her skirt and hauled herself the rest of the way up. With a final lunge, she tumbled over the railing and sprawled, panting, onto the deck. As soon as she'd caught her breath, she scrambled to her feet.

A crowd of heavily muscled blue-skinned men and women, dressed in tattered, loose-fitting tan shirts and pantaloons, encircled her. Each wore an unsheathed sword at their hip, thrust through the wide, multicolored scarves they wore as belts. Fionna eyed them warily. None of them made a move toward her, but they didn't look friendly, either. One woman with her hair pulled into a thick reddish braid hocked a truly impressive bright green loogie that splashed onto the deck inches from Fionna's bare toes.

"Oh my!" Gumball's voice came from directly behind her. Fionna whirled. Gumball and Cake floated five or six feet from the railing.

"Cake!" Fionna said. "I didn't know you could fly."

Cake's ears went flat against the side of her head. "I can't." Her voice quivered with fear.

Whatever force was levitating Gumball and Cake dumped them onto the deck beside Fionna. She helped Gumball up while Cake shrank herself to the size of a kitten and jumped onto Fionna's shoulder. Fionna, feeling Cake tremble, covered her friend with her hand, trying to comfort her.

A figure wavered into being like a mirage in front of them, and Fionna found herself nose to nose with a gray-skinned, black-haired boy. He had pointed ears and black eyes with red pupils. She hopped back a step as Gumball and Cake yelped.

"Oh my glob." Cake squashed herself against Fionna's neck. "Look at the scars on his throat, Fionna."

"Oh great," Gumball muttered. "A Vampire."

Fionna dropped into a fighting stance, wishing she'd brought her sword, and eyed the young man. Except for the pointed ears and red bite scars on his neck, he didn't look like she'd expected. No bat wings, no enormous lupine fangs, and he wasn't drooling blood. He was, however, floating several feet above the deck.

Instead of leaping on them and draining their blood, he tipped his wide-brimmed, tricorn hat and smiled at Fionna, baring a set of pointed teeth. "Hey. Welcome aboard my ship."

"It's . . . uh . . . a very nice ship. Totally nice," Fionna said.

"Thanks. I fully appreciate how awesome it is."

Gumball sniffed. "It's okay. The lines aren't as elegant as my—"

Fionna hissed and elbowed him sharply in the ribs.

"Thank you so much for rescuing us," she said

quickly, holding her hand out to the young man. "I'm Fionna, this is Cake, and this is Gum—" Just in time, she caught herself. This ship couldn't look more pirate-y if it tried, and pirates liked to kidnap rich people and princes as hostages to ransom. She coughed to cover her flub. "Er . . . this is PG."

The young man shook her hand. His skin was ice-cold and felt like it belonged to a dead slug that had been left out in a snowbank.

"Marshall Lee." He bowed dramatically and released Fionna's hand. "Pleased to meet you. Don't look so stressed. We're all very mellow here."

"You named your boat after yourself?" Disdain dripped from Gumball's tone.

"Best way to make sure people know it belongs to me," Marshall said mildly. "I don't need any squatters. You guys all look like you've been through some stuff. Come with me."

None of them budged. Marshall raised an eyebrow.

"It's only going to get colder now that the sun's going down. You really want to freeze your butts out here all night?" He turned and bobbed away from them.

"Fionna, I don't know about this," Cake whispered.

Fionna shrugged. "He's right. We don't have much choice." Without waiting to see if Gumball followed, she marched after their host.

Marshall's crew parted wordlessly before them. Fionna's nose wrinkled as she got close enough to catch a whiff of their pungent body odor. Marshall led them toward the stern. Skull-shaped lanterns bloomed with fire as he floated past. He drifted to a halt in front of a heavy wooden door that had been painted a perfect, glossy black. Fionna heard the clank of tumblers as the door unlocked itself and swung open, silently. The room beyond was pitch black. As Marshall floated across the threshold, flames flickered to life on red pillar candles that were placed on all the walls, revealing an expansive cabin.

Heavy red curtains framed a huge bay window that looked out over the night-blackened ocean. A long table, set for a lavish dinner and surrounded by high-backed wooden chairs, stood in the center of the room. Marshall floated across the table and sat in the chair at its head. With a long sigh, he leaned back, laced his fingers behind his head, and propped his booted feet on the tabletop.

"Make yourselves comfortable," he said, pushing his boots off and wiggling his toes. "You're my guests tonight."

"Such unique manners." Gumball's voice was completely flat as he gingerly sat in the chair closest to the cabin door. Fionna took the seat directly across from him.

"Oh, I'm so sorry, are things not to your liking?" Marshall asked.

Gumball sniffed. "I'm accustomed to more polite company."

"Fionna, shut him up!" Cake whispered in her left ear. "I don't want him ticking off a Vampire."

"So, Marshall," Fionna said. "What is it you do, out here?"

"Well, I'm a half-demon Vampire king, so evil, for the most part." Marshall reached up and grabbed a silk cord that dangled from the ceiling. "Making people into my minions. Stealing stuff. Writing some sick tunes. I play the guitar." He yanked on the cord. A bell tolled somewhere deep in the bowels of the ship. Instantly the cabin door flew open and two crew members came running in, each carrying a covered silver dish, along with a matching silver decanter. They set everything on the table and withdrew, shutting the door behind them. "You wanna go ahead and uncover those while I pour the wine, Princey?" he asked, levitating the decanter. Gumball's brow furrowed so deeply his eyes almost disappeared and he opened his mouth to say something.

"That's okay, I'll do it!" Cake shouted. Hunkering down even more on Fionna's shoulder, she stretched her arms out and whisked the covers off the trays, revealing a pair of huge purple octopuses. They swiveled to stare at Fionna and Cake with massive unblinking gold eyes.

"Hey, Harry," Marshall said, pulling the stopper out of the decanter. "You mind helping me out here? Marv, you hand out the food." The octopuses each made a squishy, blurbling sound. The one closest to Marshall, who Fionna assumed must be Harry, slithered off its tray, while the other pushed itself up with its tentacles, revealing a stack of fat sandwiches. Harry grabbed wine glasses and passed them to Marshall, while Marv set a sandwich on each of their plates. Fionna's stomach growled at the sight of the food. She picked up the sandwich and crammed it into her mouth. She tasted the salty-sweet of peanut butter, sliced bananas, and chocolate.

"It's good!" she said. Cake hopped off of Fionna's shoulder, grew larger, and took a tentative bite out of her own sandwich.

"It's not bad," she said grudgingly.

Marshall tipped the decanter over one of the wine goblets and thick, dark red liquid splashed into the glass.

"Tell me that's not what I think it is," Cake squeaked. Fionna's entire mouth went dry as Harry set the glass down in front of her. Gumball lifted his goblet and sniffed at its contents.

"Uhhh . . . this looks like really nice . . . uh . . ." Fionna cleared her throat and tried again. "Do you mind me asking what it is?"

Marshall grabbed a candle off the table and held it beneath his chin. It cast flickering shadows across his face that turned his eyes into solid pits of blackness. "It's . . . blood," he said, his voice low.

Gumball gasped and dropped his glass—one of

Marv's tentacles whipped out and caught it just before it hit the table.

Marshall burst out laughing. "I'm just messing with you. It's grape juice. With a twist of lime."

Cake poked Fionna in the ribs. "Laugh!" she hissed. They both tittered nervously.

Gumball scowled as he picked up his sandwich and took a bite. "What an astounding display of wittery."

Marshall lifted his glass and touched one of his pointed teeth to the side. The color drained out of the grape juice, leaving it the flat white of fresh cream. He grinned and slouched down comfortably in his chair. "You guys should go ahead and make yourselves comfortable," he said. "You don't look comfortable. Here, have a shirt."

A long-sleeved shirt flew across the room and slapped against Fionna's chest. It looked clean enough, and it was sewn from fairly thick fabric. Grudgingly, she pulled it on over her head. At least it didn't smell.

"You don't mind us crashing with you?" she asked, snagging another sandwich from Marv. She tasted cucumber, grapes, and cream cheese.

"Oh, not at all," Marshall said. "We're a pretty mellow bunch here, when we're not doing evil deeds. Don't worry, you'll have a long, long time to find out."

Fionna froze, half the sandwich sticking out of her mouth, and stared at Marshall.

Gumball set his glass down on the table with a sharp clink. "What does that mean?" he demanded.

Marshall grinned and suddenly his mouth looked very large and very full of sharp teeth. "It means you'll be staying here with me—permanently."

CHAPTER 6

Fionna leaped to her feet. "What's going on?"

"I don't pick people up out of the goodness of my heart," Marshall said. "You can pay me back," he intoned, leaning over the table and flashing his teeth, "for the rest of your lives. Muahahahahaha!"

"I knew we couldn't trust him!" Cake leaped up onto the table, grabbed for Fionna with one arm, and reached for Gumball with the other. Her arms didn't stretch. "My powers!" she cried. "I can't do anything!"

"Yeah, I took those away," Marshall said with a smug grin. "I might give them back someday. If I feel like it."

Gumball snorted and slumped down in his chair, shoulders hunched and arms folded across his chest. "I'm so not even a little surprised."

"This is totally messed up!" Fionna yelled. "Marshall, you are such a jerk!" She snatched up her plate and flung it at Marshall. The heavy china passed harmlessly through his body.

He laughed. "I can't believe you thought that was gonna work. Anyway, you may as well get started with the whole being slaves thing." He floated up out of his chair and plucked a large red guitar off a hook on the wall. "You can restring this for me. I bet Cake's whiskers would work great."

"That's it!" Fionna slammed her fist down on the table. The dishes rattled. "Marshall, I challenge you to single combat! With swords!"

"Oooo . . . ," Marshall said, setting the guitar down. "That's interesting. No one's ever done that before. I accept. But since you're the challenger, I get to make the rules." Marshall rubbed his chin. "Hmmm . . . I select . . . a race!"

Gumball groaned. "Not another one."

"Fine." Fionna snapped. "Let's get this over with."

"After you, milord," Marshall said sarcastically, sweeping another dramatic bow in front of Gumball.

The crew, who had returned to their various duties, stopped what they were doing and stared as the four of them emerged from the cabin. It was a moonless night, and Fionna didn't like to think about what kind of an edge those strange half-demon eyes would give Marshall.

Marshall pointed at the mainmast. As he lifted his hand, lanterns burst into flame all along the rigging. "Whoever gets to the top first wins."

Fionna glared at him. "All right, but no flying. You have to climb, same as me."

Marshall shrugged. "That doesn't bother me. Here, Kearney." He tossed his tricorn hat to a burly, black-bearded man. "Hold onto that for me." He arched his back and his vertebrae crackled in response. "Okay, Fionna. I'm going to be generous and give you a head start."

"You can do it, girl!" Cake said. "Kick that skinny bloodsucker's butt and get me my powers back!"

Bellowing a warrior's cry, Fionna bolted for the mainmast and swung herself up into the rigging. She pulled herself upward, planting her bare feet firmly on the ropes. They were frayed and slick with moisture. She felt a sudden, sharp tug quiver through the rigging as Marshall jumped up onto the ropes. Fionna concentrated on placing her hands, placing her feet, pulling herself up. She grabbed the next line, put her weight on it. The rope gave way beneath her hand. She yelped and clung to the solid ropes.

"You better watch it!" Marshall called to her.

Gritting her teeth, Fionna strained to reach the next highest rope. Just as her hands closed around it, the rope beneath her feet went slack. She gasped and clung to the rope, swinging back and forth, struggling to find purchase with her feet. Rope fibers bit into the palms of her hands. She held her breath and pulled her knees up to her chest, high enough that she could grab onto the rigging again with her feet. She stood, taking some of the strain off her arms.

"Hey, Fionna."

Marshall was perched on the rigging only five or six feet away. As their eyes locked, he bared his teeth and bit through the rope she was standing on, leaving her dangling again. The muscles in her arms burned in protest.

"Hey!" she shouted.

Marshall grinned. "I never said I'd make it easy for you." His grin widened as he opened his mouth and held his teeth over another rope—the one she was holding onto.

"That's it," she muttered. "I have *had* it!" She

kicked her legs as if she were on a swing, her body moving back and forth, building up speed. This time, when the rope snapped, she was ready for it. She swung outward in a perfect arc, hit the mainmast feet first, bounced off, and landed on the rigging. Her arc had put her ten feet above Marshall. As soon as she grabbed onto the ropes, she swarmed upward, climbing as fast as she could, not letting anything distract her. Her arms and legs burned with fatigue. She focused all her attention on the crow's nest and the pennant that snapped in the wind above it. Fionna sucked in a deep breath and, with one last burst of energy, leaped—

Her hands closed on the crow's nest. She'd done it. She's reached the top.

"Not bad," Marshall called up. He was still ten or so feet below her. He released the rigging and floated up to join her. "I have to admit, you did a lot better than I expected." He grabbed the back of her shirt. "I thought for sure that dress would slow you down." He plucked her off the rigging and floated them back down to the deck.

"All right." Fionna jerked out of his grip. "Now give Cake her powers back."

"Whoa," Marshall said. "Let's not get ahead of ourselves here."

Fionna glared at him. "What do you mean, Marshall?" she asked through clenched teeth. "I won fair and square."

"Right," he smirked. "You won for *you*. So I'm okay with granting you *your* freedom, but I never agreed to anything regarding those two. I'm just not feeling that generous. Besides, I need a new pillow, and I'm thinking Cake is going to be great for that."

"All right," Gumball said. "We'll challenge you, too."

"No, I'm bored now." Marshall yawned. He waved a hand, and a swathe of bright blue energy wrapped around Fionna's abdomen, squeezing the air from her lungs. She couldn't move. Marshall smiled at her as he levitated her up off the deck and swept her over the side of the ship. For one terrifying moment, she thought he was planning to dump her into the ocean, then she plopped back into the lifeboat. Fionna lay in the bottom of the boat and gasped for breath. Before she'd had a chance to recover, the single slim rope connecting the lifeboat to the *Marshall Lee* slithered back up the hull and disappeared over the railings, along with both of the lifeboat's oars.

"Bye, Fionna!" Marshall Lee called. He held Cake out over the railings, hugging her against his chest.

"Caaaaaake!" Fionna cried, leaping to her feet.

"Fionna!"

The Vampire's black-and-red eyes flashed with power, and the lifeboat shot away from the *Marshall*

Lee. The ship disappeared almost instantly into the darkness.

Fionna collapsed onto one of the benches and gripped the sides of the craft with trembling fingers. She was out in the ocean. Alone.

CHAPTER 7

Fionna kicked the side of the boat in frustration and collapsed on the rower's bench. Her anger had, at least for the moment, squashed her fear flat. She dropped her head into her hands and squeezed her eyes shut. What was she supposed to do? Marshall had taken the oars, she didn't have anything she could use as a makeshift paddle or sail, and the current was carrying her away from the *Marshall Lee* at a pretty good clip.

An image flashed through her mind, of Cake trapped in Marshall's arms, crying her name. She had to think of some way to get back.

And then we've still got to rescue all of Gumball's guests, she thought. *Glob, I never should have gone to that party, I should have stayed home . . .*

Cake would still have gone, though, and the guests would still need rescuing.

Fionna heaved a sigh. The important thing was to stay calm. She needed to think clearly. Taking a deep breath, she stood in the gently rocking craft. Maybe she could take the shirt she'd gotten from Marshall, and jury-rig some kind of a sail . . .

As she pushed her hair back, the wind died. Slowly, the waves melted into nothing, leaving the ocean's surface mirror-flat. Groaning, Fionna flopped back onto the seat.

It was a cloudless night. Every square inch of sky glittered with stars. Exhaustion washed over her. Maybe it would be best to sleep while she could. At least for the moment, she had no choice but to wait and see where the current took her. Making herself as comfortable as she could, Fionna closed her eyes.

Almost immediately, she began to dream, a jumble of terrifying images and scenes: Marshall Lee's red-and-black eyes; ocean waves as tall as trees; she climbed a net that extended straight up into the sky, and knew with the dead certainty of dream logic that she was going to have to catch a seagull once she reached the top, but no matter how long she climbed, the top never drew any closer. The scene switched, and Cake and Gumball were back in the lifeboat with her, and she was so glad to see the two of them. She laughed and hugged Cake—

She woke with a start. Something tapped against the side of the boat. As she sat up, the tapping increased in intensity. Fionna glanced over the side.

Hundreds—no, thousands—of creatures, each about the size of her hand, surrounded the boat. Each of the creatures cast a bright, yellowish-green glow that filled the water column with light. They crowded against the side of the boat, beating their heads against the hull. As she watched, a pair of the creatures hit the boards hard enough to create a pinprick leak, and a narrow stream of water arced into the boat.

Fionna gasped and slapped her hand against the leak, then tore off a scrap of cloth from her skirt and stuffed that into the hole. She leaned over the boat and slapped her hands against the water, trying to drive them away.

"Knock it off!" she shouted.

One of the creatures lifted its head from the water and stared right at her. It had huge, luminous green eyes with enormous black pupils. "Help!" it squeaked. "Help us!"

"You're gonna sink my boat!"

A huge shadow, twice the length of her boat, swept through the water beneath the creatures. Deep, primal fear shot up Fionna's spine.

"Help! Help!" the creatures squeaked in unison.

Heroes never get a break, Fionna thought.

"Hurry, get in!" She knelt in the boat and scooped handfuls of the creatures up out of the water. As the first few dropped into the bottom of the boat, the others followed, leaping out of the water and over the side, filling the boat so thickly that Fionna worried their weight would swamp the vessel.

The shadow grew larger as it rose toward the surface. Fionna scowled and curled her hands into fists. She planted her feet as firmly as she could, careful not to step on any of the keening, chittering creatures. An eyestalk poked out of the water and swiveled toward her. Without a moment's hesitation, Fionna slapped her hand across it.

A huge silver fish reared up out of the water and towered over her. Its sleek body, except for its fins, were covered in eyestalks. Every single one of its eyes pointed directly at Fionna. Scarlet flashed across the fish's skin and it opened its huge maw, revealing transparent teeth that were each as long as her arm.

"Help! Help!" The terrified creatures in the boat grabbed onto Fionna's skirt with tiny pincers.

"Let go!" Fionna staggered as she tried to brush them off. "You're gonna knock me down!"

The giant fish lunged at her. She leaped back, landing on the rear seat to avoid stepping on anyone. The fish's jaws snapped shut right over where she'd been standing.

"Back off, you bug-eyed freak," Fionna said. Instead, the fish made another try for her. Fionna punched it, striking several of its eyes, which squished unpleasantly. The fish squawked and slipped back beneath the surface, leaving nothing more sinister than ripples to betray its presence.

"Oh, thank you!" the creatures squeaked in unison. "You saved us!"

Fionna collapsed onto the seat. "Don't worry about it."

Something struck the bottom of the boat with so much force that the craft hopped out of the water. Fionna sprawled across the seat.

That fish!

The creatures in the boat began to keen and hop up and down in the air.

Fionna pulled herself to her feet. "Stay calm!" To her relief, the creatures listened, huddling into a pile at the stern.

This time, when the fish poked its head above water, Fionna was ready for it. She leaped onto its head and punched a cluster of its eyestalks. "Learn to take a hint!" she shouted. The fish screamed and flailed.

Too late, Fionna noticed just how long and flexible its fins were. One snaked around her waist and the fish threw her back into the boat. Fionna landed near one of the creatures, which flashed in alarm. The fish's nearest eyestalks flinched away from the light.

Fionna scrambled to her feet. "Flash!" she told the creatures. "As bright as you can, all together!"

For one horrible moment she was afraid the creatures wouldn't understand. Then they drew more closely together and a brilliant burst of green light exploded across her retinas, blinding her. She rubbed her eyes, blinked until the spots cleared from her vision, and saw the fish flailing back and forth, every single eyestalk pulled into its body and covered with a protective scale.

Fionna took her chance and kicked the fish in the mouth as hard as she could. Three of its teeth broke off and splashed into the water. The fish shrieked and, once again, disappeared.

"There." Fionna planted her fists on her hips. "I bet that thing's going to stay gone this time."

"Thank you!" The creatures crowded around her

feet. One, slightly larger than the others, with a yellow stripe down its abdomen, hopped onto her shoulder and rubbed itself against her cheek. "You saved us!"

Squealing, they splashed back into the water, circled the boat three times, and disappeared.

"So brave," the yellow-striped one squeaked, before it joined the others.

Fionna heaved a sigh and sank back onto the seat. As exciting as all that had been, it hadn't changed her situation. She sighed again. Maybe she should start paddling. She doubted she'd be able to get any more sleep. The thought of sticking her hands in the water bothered her less than it would have before she'd kicked that sea-monster's scaly butt.

The tapping started again.

"I'm going to rip that thing's eyes off this time," she muttered. However, as soon as she looked into the water, the tapping stopped. The group of creatures gathered into a tight mass, their lights strobing gently.

"Hero!" Yellow-stripe held something in its pincers. Fionna reached out and took it. It was one of the fish's teeth, long and slender as a fencing foil. Three of the creatures packed mud into the hole they'd made, forcing out her makeshift patch. Once they'd finished, yellow-stripe pressed its abdomen against the mud. Light flashed, and when yellow-stripe pulled away, the mud was as firm and shiny as freshly glazed ceramic. Astonished, Fionna tapped her finger against the plug. It felt like stone. Fionna grinned. "Wow, thanks."

"Never forget you," yellow-stripe purred.

"No, never!" the others agreed. With a final flash of light, they disappeared again.

CHAPTER 8

After an hour of using her hands to paddle, Fionna gave up. All her effort was getting her nowhere fast. She was hot, tired, and thirsty, and her skin itched from the saltwater. She'd have to think of something else. She picked up the giant tooth and turned it over and over, watching it gleam in the gathering dawn. At least she'd gotten something cool out of this whole mess. She couldn't wait to show it to Cake. They'd hang it on the wall in their tree house, right across from the couch.

A breath of wind slipped across her cheeks. Fionna lifted her head, scratching absently at the salt dried onto her neck. Clouds were massing on the eastern horizon. The sun rose a few fingers above the water before the clouds blotted it out. Fionna shivered and rubbed her arms as the breeze grew stronger, teasing wavelets from the ocean's surface, and pushing the cloud bank toward her. Gray streamers of rain, like smudges of charcoal, darkened the air beneath the clouds. Lightning flickered deep within the clouds, and Fionna counted the seconds until the peal of thunder reached her ears.

Not just clouds.

An entire swarm of flying jellyfish, each at least as big as a truck, floated toward her, their scalloped, deceptively delicate-looking tendrils trailing inches from the water's surface. Fionna's stomach roiled. The last thing she needed was to get caught in an electrical storm full of poisonous jellyfish. Quickly, she unlaced her skirt and stepped out of it, grateful for the giant pair of bloomers she'd decided to wear.

She tore the skirt down the middle, tied a corner to each of her ankles, and knotted the other two corners around her wrists. Facing into the wind, she spread her arms and legs. Her heart pounded as she waited to see if her idea would work.

At first almost nothing happened. Wind filled the makeshift sail, and Fionna could feel the fabric strain against her limbs. She held her breath. Then, slowly, the boat picked up speed. She let out a delighted whoop as she skimmed across the waves. Now she was getting somewhere. She'd head for shore, get someone to help her track down Cake and Gumball, and then they'd rescue the hostages. If she could just stay ahead of the storm—

The boat coasted to a stop. Fionna froze, dumbfounded. The wind was steady, her sail billowed around her—what was the problem? Brown kelp floated in the water, but the mats certainly didn't appear thick enough to block her boat.

Something slapped against the stern, and Fionna whirled toward it. A leaf. A flat tan kelp leaf slipped over the boat's side. It slithered across the bottom, moving toward her. Several more followed, dragging their long stems behind them.

"Oh great!" Fionna snatched up the fish tooth and hopped up onto the seat, away from the kelp.

The mass of kelp gathered together, stalks and leaves and translucent floats writhing and twisting. It took on a vaguely humanoid shape. A mouth opened in the lumpy, misshapen head. A horrible rotten fish smell washed over her. "Stay with us," the thing said, in a voice like leaves rustling.

She growled in frustration. She didn't have time to dance around with a flipping kelp monster.

She speared one of the floats and it sprayed green liquid across her. The stems were knotty and fibrous, much tougher than their translucent appearance had led her to expect.

More and more stalks whipped over the sides of the boat. Fionna slashed at them with the fish tooth. Sticky gold sap splashed across her face each time she cut through one of the stalks. A cold, wet leaf slapped itself around her ankle. It burned— she cried out and ripped it off.

"Quit being a creeper!" Fionna snapped. "Glob, you make the Ice Queen look well-adjusted."

"We're hungry and lonely," the kelp person rustled. "Mostly hungry."

"That is so it!" Fionna kicked the kelp person in the head. "This ocean is totally the worst place ever! When I get back on dry land, I'm going to kick Gumball's butt for inviting me to his stupid lousy party in the first place." She rained blows on the kelp, driving it back. Tattered leaves fluttered through the air. "Go find someone else to eat and get off my boat!"

"I'm a prince. You be my princess. I promise

not to eat you for at least a week. No matter how much I want to."

"How desperate do you think I am? Not even if you weren't the creepiest, grossest, burniest plant monster in all of Ooo."

"So mean," it moaned. "So lonely . . . so hungry."

Fionna set her jaw and kicked it in the chest as hard as she could. It flew backward and landed in the water with a huge splash. "That's not my problem." Panting, she waited until the water smoothed and she was sure the kelp monster wasn't coming back. Finally, she risked a glance over her shoulder. The storm and the jellyfish were so close she could make out the fringe of pink frills on each dangling tentacle.

Her skirt-sail was covered with sap. Useless. Disgusted, she tugged it off, wadded it into a ball, and threw it into the bottom of the boat. Lightning flashed again. A few raindrops splashed against her cheeks. Just as the first deafening peal of thunder hit, the sky opened. Rain pounded into the water in thick sheets, slashing her visibility down to nothing. The wind howled and whipped at her clothing, driving the rain against her. The waves surged and knocked her off her feet. She clung to the side of the boat as waves slapped against the craft, hitting it broadside. Water poured over the sides and pooled around her legs.

A jellyfish tendril swung at her out of the chaos. Fionna cried out and jerked away from it just as another huge wave crashed into her chest and knocked her out of the boat. Limbs windmilling, she hit the surface. Waves closed over her head. The fish tooth slipped from her fingers as she fought her way back to the surface. Waves slapped against her face, driving water up her nose. She choked, coughed, and paddled frantically at the water. Lightning strikes flashed all around her, searing her retinas. Streamers of kelp slipped past her, and Fionna snatched at them as she struggled to keep her head above water. She couldn't grab a stalk, and her fingers tore through the leaves. Another wave washed across the top of her head, driving her down into the water. Heart pounding, she kicked frantically for the surface. Her eyes stung and the bitter tang of salt filled her mouth as she choked and gasped.

One of the jellyfish floated directly overhead, its bell so huge it blocked her entire field of vision. Fionna screamed as the tentacles surrounded her, tangling around her limbs. She reared back, trying to break free. More tentacles surrounded her, pulling her up out of the water.

And nothing was hurting her. The realization struck her so sharply that she froze, shocked into immobility. The tentacles weren't stinging her. And the cold—she was completely soaked, she should have been freezing, but she wasn't. She felt fine. Her left arm was free, and she brought it up close to her face. Her skin gleamed, but not with water. The sap—it hadn't washed off of her and it coated her like a second skin.

It was insulating her!

Without questioning her good luck, Fionna wrapped the tentacle around her left leg, locking it beneath her feet. She climbed, hand over hand, pushing herself up. The tentacles thickened the closer she climbed to the jellyfish's bell, offering her protection from the wind. The jellyfish's dome glowed ever so slightly with a pale pink light. Lightning flashes illuminated the creature, and Fionna could see dark objects swimming lazily through the stomach pouch. She lifted a hand, pressing it against the underside of the dome. The jellyfish's skin felt as stretchy and pliable as a balloon. One of the dark objects seemed to take notice of her—it slowed and drifted toward her. Fionna licked her lips, tasting salt. Every muscle in her body tense and trembling, she waited to see what would happen.

The dark object pressed closer, becoming clearer as the jellyfish's skin thinned around it. An eye the size of a basketball stared down at her. It had a slit pupil and a deep crimson iris. Fionna stared back at it. For some reason she didn't feel afraid. Slowly, the eye drew back. The jellyfish's skin welled around Fionna's hand, pushing down around her arm. It felt warm and somehow comforting. She squeezed her eyes shut, held her breath, and stayed perfectly still as it surrounded her head.

CHAPTER 9

It was utterly silent inside the bell. Carefully, Fionna cracked open her eyelids. Six inky-black fishlike things with long, delicately fringed feathers and huge unblinking eyes floated languidly around her. None of them took the slightest interest in her. One bumped lightly into the side of her head, before it bounced off and continued on its way.

The jellyfish's skin expanded to encompass her entire body. She stood, placing one hand against the side of the bell to steady herself. The only sound was the soft patter of water dripping off her clothes. The air was warm and smelled of roses, though not overpoweringly so. The sides of the bell breathed in and out ever so slightly.

Her legs trembled with sudden exhaustion. She sank down, then flopped onto her back. She couldn't run or fight or swim or plan any longer. The relief of being somewhere that wasn't the ocean was immense. She closed her eyes and took a deep breath. More than anything, she wished she were back home in her bed, snuggled down warm and safe under her pile of faux furs, with Cake asleep in the dresser drawer beside her.

When she opened her eyes, one of the black fish things was floating almost directly above her face. It stared down at her, the tips of its feathers quivering. It radiated tranquility. One of its feathers dipped down and touched her forehead.

A heavy, comforting weight settled over her body. She glanced down. A blanket had appeared on top of her—and not just any blanket, *her* blanket, her favorite from home. She sat up in shock, clutching at the fur. It looked right, felt right, even smelled faintly of stale meatloaf. She glanced back at the fish thing.

"You know what I'd really like?" She enunciated each word carefully. "A cup of hot energy drink. Honey flavor. With whipped cream. And sprinkles. And marshmallows."

The fish thing touched her forehead again and a steaming mug appeared in front of her eyes. Fionna reached up and wrapped her hand around it. It was warm, and the fragrant steam filled her nostrils as she took a deep breath.

"Wow." Fionna ran a finger around the rim of the mug. "I wish . . . Cake was here," she said slowly.

A dark shape grew out of the floor. Slowly it changed shape. It grew pointed ears and a pair of almond-shaped eyes in a face that was a pretty good likeness of Cake's. Then it slumped to the side. Three arms extended out of its sides and tails grew the entire length of its spine. Maybe it was having trouble mimicking both Cake and her shape-changing abilities. Its mouth melted as it opened.

"Bleeeeeeeeeeeeeeeeee," it said as its jaw pooled on its liquescent feet.

"Oh dag, forget it. Thanks but no thanks. I don't want to see Cake anymore." Cake's form melted back into the jellyfish's side.

"Hmmm . . ." Fionna glanced at the fish thing as she slipped off her hood and wrung out her hair. "Do Gumball, but with three heads. And make him sing."

Gumball's lanky body grew up out of the floor. For a minute he stood there, handsome and regal looking. Bulbous growths developed on his head, one on each side, just above his ears, and each of the growths turned into a new head. Each of the heads' mouths opened and a warbling birdsong emerged from their throats.

Fionna took a sip of her drink. "This is so wrong."

She waved her hand. "Okay, enough, enough. I . . . probably shouldn't tell anybody about this."

She pulled the blanket around her shoulders, tucked her legs up to her chest, set the mug on her kneecaps, and thought. Anything she asked for appeared, more or less. Though the jellyfish seemed to have less trouble with inanimate objects than people. Cake and Gumball certainly hadn't been real, though thankfully her blanket and drink appeared to be. She frowned and watched the fish things. She counted them. There were ten. But when she'd first entered the jellyfish's bell, hadn't she only counted six? Where had the other four come from?

One of the fish things floated to the side of the bell, brushed up against it, quickly sank into the pinkish flesh, and disappeared. Fionna's eyes widened. She'd thought the fish things were independent organisms, perhaps some kind of parasite, but were they actually part of the jellyfish, like blood cells or boogers? She downed the rest of her drink and squashed a series of tiny Marshall Lees that she conjured up out of the floor. If she could control the inside of the jellyfish, was it possible she could control the outside as well? She jammed her thumb down onto one last Marshall Lee and set down her mug. As soon as she let go, it disappeared into the floor. The same thing happened when she set down the blanket. She stood and willed a plushy green chair into existence, then sank back onto its cushions with a sigh.

"How about a window?" she said, stretching her arms out on the padded armrests. A large picture window opened in the jellyfish's flesh. Outside, the storm raged on, lightning and rain and wind, and thank glob she wasn't stuck out in the middle of that mess anymore.

A tray table swelled up out of the floor and produced a paper bowl full of fresh french fries. The jellyfish was still floating along, tentacles trailing through the water. Fionna crammed a fistful of fries into her mouth. They were perfect—crispy, mealy, hot, with a dash of salt and the subtle heat of garlic. Her thoughts raced as she chewed, swallowed, and stuffed more fries into her mouth. She only needed to know one thing: was the jellyfish completely dependent on the wind, or could it move under its own power? Fionna wiped her greasy fingers on her shirt and leaned forward in her seat.

"Go up," she whispered.

There was a pause, and then the ocean began to recede.

"Yes!" Fionna shouted. "Go to the right." Slowly, the jellyfish moved in the correct direction. She took a breath. "Okay, jellyfish. Do you know where my friends are?"

The jellyfish hung, wavering, in the sky, as if processing her request. Would it be able to do what she wanted? Could it find something in the real world? Maybe it could only create copies.

A fish thing floated up to Fionna and rested one of its feathers on top of her head. After a moment, the others swam a lazy circuit around the inside of the bell. They came to a stop almost directly behind Fionna. The jellyfish swung around, its window turning to face the direction the fish things had indicated. The storm was finally starting to break up and streams of light poked through the thinning clouds. East. A red arrow formed on the window, pointing slightly to the right.

Fionna jumped up out of her chair. "Mathematical!" A gracefully curved pink crystal saber sprouted like a sapling from the floor beside her. She grabbed it. It was as light as a feather, with perfect balance. She brandished it at the window. "Take me to the *Marshall Lee!*"

CHAPTER 10

The jellyfish flew at a speed that surpassed Fionna's wildest expectations. In less than an hour, they floated above Marshall's ship, which had dropped anchor in a cove between two small sandy islands. A hole opened in the center of the floor, and Fionna knelt beside it, staring down at the *Marshall Lee*. The pale blue water glittered in the sunlight. She didn't see anyone on deck—she supposed it was possible that Marshall and his crew slept during the day. She'd assumed his crew was alive, but they could just as easily be ghouls. Fionna frowned as she considered her options.

On the one hand, it might not be a bad idea to keep the jellyfish handy, in case she needed anything else. But on the other hand, she didn't like the idea of keeping it separated from its swarm longer than was necessary. Besides, it wasn't like she could count on the plant sap to protect her forever.

Fionna checked the sword she'd slung across her back to make sure the straps were secure. "I guess I'm gonna head out now." She patted one of the fish things on the head. "Thanks for everything, dude."

She glanced at her hands, evaluating how much of the sap remained. Enough to protect her as she climbed down?

A pair of brown leather gloves popped out of the floor beside her. Fionna grinned. "You're the best!" She slipped them on—they fit perfectly—leaped out through the hole, grabbed onto one of the tentacles, and slid smoothly down it. She landed in the water with a splash.

There was no reaction from aboard the ship. No one poked their head over the railing or raised an alarm. Marshall obviously hadn't bothered to set any lookouts.

"Arrogant," Fionna muttered as she let go of the tentacle. Treading water, she waved good-bye to the jellyfish. It floated away, back up into the sky, while Fionna breaststroked to the anchor and grabbed onto the thick, barnacle-encrusted chain. The water was practically balmy, as warm as bathwater, and so clear she could see straight down to the clean white sand interspersed with mounds of pink and blue coral. She refused to think about what might be in the water with her. Placing her hands carefully to avoid cutting her palms on the barnacles, she shimmied up the anchor, then its chain, and flipped herself up over the railing. She landed on one of the lower decks. She crouched on the sun-warmed planks, heart pounding.

No one came to investigate. All she heard were

the ship's creaks and groans.

She scrambled to her feet and flattened herself against the wall. She had to find Cake and Gumball. She crept to the first door, took a breath, and wrapped her hand around the cool brass knob. She was on the ship's sunward side—she felt braver with the light on her back. She twisted the knob gently to the right. The door swung open a few inches. Fionna peered inside. Light fell around her, into the darkened room. It took a minute for her eyes to adjust, and when they finally did, all she saw were stacks of wooden crates. "Cake!" she whispered. "PG!" No one answered. Fionna shut the door and thought. She couldn't very well check every single room on every single level of this boat. It would take forever and, unless she got very lucky, she'd probably get caught before she managed to find her friends. It wasn't going to stay light forever. She guessed she had maybe another three hours before nightfall.

Fionna chewed her lower lip. Wait. What was it Marshall had said when he'd taunted her? He'd mentioned needing a new pillow. Her stomach sank. Suddenly she knew, without a shadow of a doubt, where Cake was.

She glanced at the sun. As long as there was daylight, there was a good chance she could get one over on Marshall.

Probably. Maybe. If she was lucky.

"Yeah, super lucky," she muttered.

But what was her alternative? Find Gumball first, and see if he could help her? He hadn't exactly struck her as a rough and tumble kind of guy. What could he do—bake Marshall to death?

Baking . . . Marshall had seemed like a practical person, at least as far as half-demon Vampire kings went. He'd probably assigned Gumball to the galley.

It was worth a look, she decided. Chances were she'd find the galley long before she reached Marshall's cabin. And who knew, maybe she was being unfair to Gumball. He might not turn out to be as useless as she'd anticipated. After all, he'd been pretty handy with the survival gear when they'd been stuck in the lifeboat. She closed her eyes and took a deep breath, sucking air through her nostrils, searching for anything that smelled like food.

At first all she could smell was saltwater and warm, oiled wood. Then, so subtly that at first she almost missed it, she caught a whiff of something warm and sugary. Baking cakes.

She drew her sword and ran, following that thread of scent. It led her along the side of the ship, up one level, and straight to the doors of the galley. She peeked in through the blue double doors and saw Gumball, alone, and hard at work stirring a batch of pink batter in a big orange bowl.

"Algebraic!" she whispered. It was so *awesome* when her hunches turned out to be correct. "Hey, PG!"

Gumball dropped the bowl onto the floor. It shattered with a huge crash, spattering his legs with batter. "Fionna!" he exclaimed. "What are you doing here? Where'd you get that sword? And what are you covered in?"

"Glob, Gumball, shut up!" Fionna said, rushing into the galley and pulling the doors shut behind her. "Where is everybody? Asleep?"

Gumball nodded. "They all turned in a little before sunrise."

"What about Cake?"

Gumball shrugged. "I'm not sure. Marshall took her with him."

Great. Just what she'd been afraid of.

"Okay, get over here, and let's go get her, and then get the hell out of here."

"That would be awesome, but there's one problem." Gumball lifted his right leg, and only then did Fionna realize he was chained to a big staple that had been driven into the wall. Fionna groaned and knelt beside him, examining the thick iron shackle.

"There's no keyhole," Gumball said, "or I definitely could have picked it by now. I know a lot about locks." He grabbed her gloved hand as she reached out to touch the smooth band. "Be careful. I think it's magic. I tried to chip at it with a knife a couple of times and it shocked me."

Fionna stood and held her sword out over the chain. "Let's see if this'll do the trick."

Gumball's eyes widened. "Hey, wait," he said as she drew back for her swing. "Are you sure that's the best—"

The blade came whistling down, struck the chain and, in a shower of white sparks, sliced it cleanly in two. Gumball yelped and stiffened as the sparks shot up his body, before dissipating off the top of his head.

"Ooo, sorry," Fionna said. Every strand of

Gumball's pink hair stood on end. "You okay?"

Gumball's teeth chattered. "F-f-f-fine." Fionna smelled something like sugar burning. Wisps of smoke rose from his head. Fionna patted at his hair, trying to smooth it back down. It felt like straw.

"Little conditioner, I bet it'll be fine," she said with a weak smile. "Can you walk?"

Gumball took a few stiff, halting steps, then reeled into the table.

"Hey there!" Fionna grabbed at his arm, pulling him back onto his feet. "Good thing that was bolted down, huh?" Fionna slung Gumball's arm over her shoulder and dragged him toward the galley doors. She propped him against the wall and dashed over to a stool with narrow, spindled legs. It had been screwed into the floor near one of the counters. She chopped at the legs with her sword, hacking the stool to pieces.

"Fionna, what are you going to do? Even if we

get Cake, we're still stuck on this boat."

"It's daytime." Fionna sheathed her sword and picked the longest, most jaggedy-ended piece of wood from the pile. "I'm gonna stab me a Vampire."

CHAPTER 11

"This is a bad idea, Fionna," Gumball whispered. They stood before the door to Marshall Lee's cabin.

Fionna hefted the stool leg. "It'll work. Once I've staked Marshall, his ghouls will keel over dead, too, and we can take over the ship."

Gumball swayed a bit. He gripped the doorframe to steady himself. "Have you killed a Vampire before?"

Fionna rolled her eyes. "No, but I've read a lot about it."

Gumball coughed. "Touché."

"Just wait here and stay quiet."

"I'm not an idiot. I think I can manage both those things."

Fionna eyed Gumball. "Just don't be a hero." Holding her rudimentary stake out in front of her, she gripped the doorknob. "I'll be right back." She pushed the door open a few inches, slipped inside, and let it swing shut behind her. It was nearly pitch black inside. She held her breath. She heard low, steady breathing.

Marshall.

She blinked and the blackness separated into different shades of gray. Fionna crept forward, skirting around the long table and chairs, careful not to bump into anything. She remembered there being a berth toward the back of the room, directly underneath the huge picture window. It was possible Marshall slept like a bat hanging from the ceiling, but then why even bother having a bed? She inched forward another couple of inches, coming in sight of the bed, and froze.

Heavy velvet curtains covered the picture window. In the thick shadows below, Marshall lay in bed, tucked under a patched quilt. Just as she'd feared, his head rested smack on the middle of Cake's pudgy back. Cake's arms dangled over the edge of the bed.

"Cake," Fionna whispered. Cake's eyes opened. Fionna grinned and pointed at the stake, then made a few quick stabbing motions in the air. Cake's eyes widened. Fionna tiptoed forward and stood over Marshall. His chest rose and fell. Her hand felt hot and sweaty around the stake. Could she really stab someone to death in their sleep, even if he was a self-professed super evil, half-demon Vampire king?

"Oh schlub, how much longer are you going to stand there?" Marshall asked, opening his eyes. Fionna yelped and stumbled back as he sat up. He yawned and stretched. "You're seriously mucking with my beauty sleep."

"H-how long have you been—"

"Awake? Since you opened the door." Marshall pushed back the covers and, in one smooth motion, hopped out of bed, Cake tucked under his arm. He plucked the stake from Fionna's nerveless fingers. "You want to surprise a freakin' Vampire king, you're going to have to get a lot better at sneaking around. You sound like a herd of elephants."

Fionna flushed and ripped her sword from its sheath.

"Oh please." Marshall sighed, tossed the stake over his shoulder onto the bed, and flicked his fingers. Fionna's sword wrenched itself out of her hands and slammed point first into the wall. He smiled, radiating smugness. "It's going to take more than that to put a dent in the chiseled perfection of my exterior."

Just then, the door crashed against the wall. Gumball, flailing his arms over his head, lurched into the cabin. Marshall Lee hissed and fell back.

Fionna took her chance—she lunged across Marshall's bed, grabbed a fistful of drape, and yanked as hard as she could. There was the soft purr of cloth tearing, then late-day sunlight flooded the room as the drape crumpled across the bed.

Howling, Marshall Lee bent double, hands pressed against his eyes. Wherever the sun touched him, his skin sizzled and smoked like pork in a frying pan.

Fionna grabbed Cake's hands, yanked her away from Marshall, and ran for the door. "Gumball, come on! Let's get out of here!"

Gumball tottered after her, and too late she realized how stiff his legs still were. He slammed into her, tripping them both up. They tumbled out onto the deck. Cake spun out of Fionna's grip and landed on her feet. She turned toward the door.

"Hah, you stupid Vampire!" she shouted. "Come and get us now, while we're out in the sun! Yeah, I didn't think so!"

"Cake, knock it off!" Fionna pushed herself to her feet. She grabbed Gumball's arm, dragging him up beside her. "Help me with him, and let's just get out of here."

"You really think it's going to be that easy?" The deep, gravelly voice sent chills up Fionna's spine. She glanced back into the cabin. Marshall stood in a patch of deep shade just a few feet from the doorway. His eyes glowed red out of a face that had changed in some strange, incomprehensible way. His nose looked flatter, his mouth wider. His breath wheezed in and out of his lungs. The places on his face, neck, and arms where the sun had touched him were red and covered with weeping blisters. A pair of black bat wings rose from his shoulder blades and arched over his head as his eyes sank into their sockets. "I was willing to cut you some slack because it impressed me that you managed to get back here, but you've really angered me." He took a step forward and as he moved his back hunched, pushing his head forward on his neck. His nails grew into long black claws. "I think maybe I'm going to turn you into a ghoul." He waved his hand. Magical energy rushed toward her. Fionna cried out and lifted her arms.

The energy washed over and around her, but didn't harm her. Sparks skated harmlessly across her skin. Astonished, she lifted her head. Marshall looked equally shocked.

The plant sap! It was still protecting her!

Fionna leaped at Marshall and punched him square in his squat, batlike nose. He grabbed his face and reeled away from her.

"Hey! Ow! Okay, truce, truce!" Marshall glared at her as he clamped his hands around his nose. "Great, I'm bleeding. That really skrogged my snot-cellar. You want to hand me that red book over there?"

Fionna glanced at the book, which was lying on a small table a few feet to her right. She glanced back at Marshall. His wings and claws had disappeared. He stood with his eyes squinched shut, head tilted back, pinching the bridge of his nose. Setting her jaw, Fionna marched past him, yanked her sword out of the wall, then grabbed the book and handed it to him.

"Fionna, what are you doing?" Cake gasped. "He was just about to eat us or make us into ghouls or whatever and you're *helping* him?" She slapped a hand across her forehead.

"Well, come on, it's not like he's going to do anything now," Fionna said.

Cake scowled and her arm stretched out and wrapped around Fionna's waist. "Hey! My powers are back!" Grinning, she yanked Fionna out onto the deck.

"Yeah, I figured those would be showing up again soon." Marshall heaved a sigh. "I spiked your food with some medicine that takes a person's magic away for a day or so. I was planning on putting more in your breakfast." He stuck the book into his mouth.

The red covers drained to white. "Oh well. It's too bad, you're a really great pillow. First time in forever I woke up without a crick in my neck." He let go of his nose, sniffed hard, and wiped his hand on his pants.

"If you've got your powers back, let's cut our losses here already," Gumball said. "I've had it with this ship. Just turn into a really big balloon or something and fly us back to port."

Cake's tail poufed with anger. "I told you, I can't carry the both of you at the same time. And anyway, what about all the people the Ice Queen kidnapped? What about my sweet baby, Lord Monochromicorn? They're all depending on us. If we could go flying off somewhere, it'd be after them."

"Yeah," Fionna said.

"Sounds like maybe you guys could use a little help," Marshall interjected.

Fionna raised an eyebrow. "Help. From you. Why would you do that?"

Marshall stuck his hands into his pockets and floated into a reclined position. "This is pretty much the most fun I've had in about three hundred years or so. Being immortal is flipping boring 98 percent of the time. I'd love to keep this excitement going. And besides, the Ice Queen and I had a thing about eight hundred years ago. Long story short, we were roomies, she ate a bunch of my food and never paid me back, I'd really like to settle that hash with her, and I'm willing to help you dweebs to do it."

"What about your crew?" Fionna asked. "Will they go along with that?"

"Oh, you don't have to worry about them." Marshall waved his hand. "They're not real. Just a bunch of illusions. I told you, immortality is boring. So how about it? You gonna let me help you or what?"

Fionna, Gumball, and Cake exchanged glances.

"Mathematical?" Fionna said.

CHAPTER 12

"The Ice Queen is right up ahead." Marshall ducked down in the crow's nest and handed Fionna his spyglass. He reached up under the wide brim of his straw sun-hat and scratched at his forehead. "She's just sitting there."

Fionna brought the glass up to her eye and adjusted the focus. The sun was almost directly overhead, and there was a fine haze of cloud, just enough to cut down the glare off the water. The queen's ship filled her field of vision. Fionna trained the spyglass along the ship—the prisoners were still in their pen on the main deck—and the Ice Queen sat on a beach chair at the bow of the ship. Her head was tilted back, and Fionna thought she might be asleep.

"I don't get it," Cake muttered from her perch on top of Fionna's head.

Fionna scowled and lowered the glass. "She's waiting for us. She doesn't just want to beat us, she wants us to *see* her beat us."

Cake snorted. "That is one messed-up mind, there."

Marshall scratched his face again. Most of his sun blisters had faded, but his skin was still flushed and peeling.

"Er, sorry about your face and stuff," Fionna said. "That whole trying to burn you alive thing."

"Don't worry about it." Marshall grinned. "It takes more than that to permanently muck up all this man-pretty. Besides, it's only fair. I did set you adrift in a boat with no supplies. Sorry about that, by the way."

"This is all super cute," Cake snapped. "But can you guys save the goo-goo eyes for later? What's our plan?"

"Marshall, you said we're not far from the Island Guy, right?"

Marshall nodded. "Maybe ten, twenty minutes tops, with clear sailing. Weather's perfect today."

Fionna pursed her lips. "All right then. We'll sneak up and cut right across her bow. Then we'll come around hard and stay in front of her. We'll block her."

Marshall nodded. "Sounds like a plan."

Cake grabbed Fionna, stepped over the side of the crow's nest with a rapidly elongating leg, and carried them both down to the deck, while Marshall drifted down beside them.

"Go help Gumball," Fionna told Cake.

"You be careful, Fionna," Cake said. "I don't want you getting all iced up."

Fionna smiled, doing her best to project a confidence she wasn't sure she felt. "Don't worry. I got this all under control."

Marshall waved his hands as Cake ran into the galley behind them. A huge gust of wind filled the sails. The ship leaped forward so suddenly Fionna staggered against the railing. She steadied herself, craning her neck to keep the queen's ship squarely in her sights. They skimmed across the waves, closing on the queen's ship. Fionna's heartbeat pounded in her throat—the Ice Queen still hadn't seen them. Maybe they'd be able to get the drop on her.

"Oh my glob!" Lumpy Space Prince's voice carried clearly across the water. "Fionna, is that you? Like, hurry up and lumping rescue us already!"

Fionna groaned and smacked herself in the forehead as the Ice Queen leaped up from her beach chair.

"Well, that's not helpful," Marshall said.

"There you are!" the Ice Queen shouted. She swooped into the air and hovered above Fionna and Marshall. "I knew you'd be along sooner or later. Where's Gumball? And who's your little friend?"

Marshall tilted his head back, careful to keep the brim of his hat turned toward the sun. "Long time no see, Icey."

"Ugh! Marshall Lee. You were the worst roommate ever! Always keeping track of every little thing! Who cares who ate the last ice-cream sandwich?" She glared at Fionna. "I'm so not surprised you're hanging out with someone like him. Now quit wasting my time. Where's Gumball? Hand him over and maybe I won't turn you into a blond Popsicle."

"So not gonna happen." Fionna drew her sword and leveled the blade at the Ice Queen. "This race isn't over yet."

"Oh whatever." Laughing, the Ice Queen sprayed the water around the *Marshall Lee* with her magic, freezing it instantly into a solid, glittering sheet of ice. The ship shuddered to a stop, its timbers groaning.

"You are such a big stinking cheat!" Fionna shouted. "That's it—the gloves are coming off right freakin' now! Cake, Gumball, Plan B!"

Gumball and Cake ran out of the galley, carrying a giant, four-tiered, red-and-white cake decorated with tiny hearts.

"Gumball!" The queen looked delighted.

"Lock and load," Cake said. She hugged the enormous pastry to her chest while Fionna and Marshall each grabbed one of her legs and braced themselves against the railing. Before the queen had a chance to react, Gumball gripped Cake's shoulders and pulled back, turning her body into a giant slingshot.

"Fire!" Fionna said.

With a grunt, Gumball let go, and Cake's body snapped forward. "Eat cake!" she shouted, opening her arms. The pastry flew through the air and struck the Ice Queen, exploding across her face and upper body. The Ice Queen squawked as the force of the blow slammed her into the thick ice. A chorus of cheers rose from the queen's vessel, with a fierce "neigh" nearly drowning out the other voices.

"We're coming, baby!" Cake shouted. "Just hang on!"

"Ahhh!" the Ice Queen screamed. "It burns!"

Gumball beamed. "That's because it's filled with triple-strength dragon-fart chilis."

"Four hundred thousand on the Marshall Lee scale of mouth-searingly screaming hotness," Marshall said. "I believe in the virtues of a well-stocked larder."

Groaning, the Ice Queen blasted her face clean with slush and blinked up at Fionna out of enraged, bloodshot eyes. "Not fair!" she yelled. "We never agreed to chemical warfare."

Fionna sneered down at her. "You should have

thought of that before you started cheating." She waved her sword. "Rapid fire!"

Gumball ran back into the galley and returned carrying a basket full of purple cupcakes. Cake windmilled her arms as Gumball and Fionna dropped cupcakes into her hands. The tiny projectiles battered the queen, spattering her dress with their cream-filled guts as she raised her arms in a futile attempt to block them.

Fionna leaped onto the railing, grabbed a nearby rope, and slashed it with her sword. "Cover me!" she said. As a fusillade of cupcakes whizzed through the air around her, she swung down onto the ice, rolled, and hopped to her feet with her sword in a guard position across her torso.

The Ice Queen wiped frosting out of her hair and glared at Fionna. "I'm going to smash you into next week, you putrid blond parsnip."

Magic crackled through the air. A jagged ice wall

erupted behind Fionna, cutting her off from the ship. She tightened her grip on her sword. "Let's do this."

The Ice Queen's arm shot out and she hurled an ice ball the size of her head at Fionna. Fionna gasped and moved her weapon to block it. A single clear, pure tone rang through the air when the ice struck the blade, the vibration numbing Fionna's hands. She darted to the side, her feet sliding across the ice. She jammed her sword into the ice and, using it as an anchor, let her momentum swing her around behind the Ice Queen. Before she could take advantage of her position, a waist-high sheet of ice surged between them. The Ice Queen flailed and struggled to turn around, her legs tangling in her heavy skirts. "Quit moving around so much!" she snapped.

Fionna sprang onto the top of the wall, feinted left, and kicked at the queen's head, aiming for her crown. The queen ducked to the side, staying just out of reach. With a snarl, she encased Fionna's feet in a thick layer of ice, freezing them to the wall. "I said stay put!"

"You're gonna have to do better than that," Fionna said. She flipped back off the wall and her feet popped out of her boots, which she'd borrowed from Marshall, and were a size too big. She ducked down behind the wall just as a curtain of sleet ripped through the air where she'd been standing. She scrambled around the wall, heading for her sword. She skated toward her weapon, her feet struggling for purchase on the slick ice.

"Not so fast!" An ice floe slipped past her and enveloped her sword. Fionna backpedaled furiously, but her feet shot out from under her and she skidded into it. Panting, she flopped onto her stomach and pushed herself up onto her hands and knees.

"Any last words?" The Ice Queen loomed over her. She raised her hands, her eyes sparkling. "I'd say I'm sorry things turned out this way but . . . I'm not." Almost languidly, she waved her hands.

Nothing happened.

The Ice Queen gasped and fell back a pace, and as she did so, her crown slipped off her head and hung in the air. The queen's jaw dropped.

"No!" she shouted, slapping her hands down on the top of her head. "My crown!"

The crown whisked away from her, stopping just above Fionna.

"Good job, Marshall," she said.

"No problem." Grinning, Marshall materialized beside Fionna and held out the crown. Fionna took it, surprised at its weight. The gold was warm, not cold as she'd expected.

"Augh! You're the worst!" The queen sobbed in frustration.

Fionna smirked. "That'll learn you about your creepy-weirdo man stalking."

"You guys okay down there?" Gumball called down from the ship.

Fionna waved the crown above her head, its apple-red gems gleaming. "We're fine." She smiled at Marshall. "We've got this all under control."

CHAPTER 13

The scent of freshly baked banana bread wafted across the Island Guy as Fionna sighed and lay back on the warm sand. Cake had stretched herself as an awning over herself, Marshall, and Lord Monochromicorn, and all four watched as Gumball pulled steaming loaves from the portable stove they'd set up on the beach. The party guests frolicked in the surf, laughing and splashing one another. Even Lumpy Space Prince was having a good time, collecting shells.

"How's it going down there?" the Island Guy boomed.

"It's great, thanks!" Fionna said.

"Augh!" Pacing the shoreline, the Ice Queen flung a handful of kelp back into the ocean. "It's not here, either!"

Fionna dug her toes into the sand and closed her eyes, listening to the Island Guy's palm fronds rustle in the lazy tropical breezes. "Any chance of her finding that crown anytime soon?" she asked.

Marshall adjusted his sunglasses and pillowed his head on his arms. "I wouldn't worry about it. I hid it pretty well."

"Yeah? What'd you do with it?"

"Buried it under my beach towel."

"Nice."

"We should kick that thing into the ocean and get rid of it for good," Cake grumbled.

"Aw, now Cake." Fionna reached up and tickled Cake's stomach. "Be nice. I'm sure she'll find it eventually after we're gone."

Whistling, Gumball marched up to them carrying three loaves of his bread on banana leaf trays. "Hot and fresh and full of yum," he said, plopping down beside them.

"That smells great." Fionna took a slice and sank her teeth into the warm bread.

"I got one just for you, Marshall," Gumball said, handing Marshall a loaf slathered with red frosting.

"Mmmm, thanks," Marshall said. He drained the color with a grin.

Fionna finished her bread, licked her fingers, and scanned the beach. "You know, the sun'll be down soon. You guys want to go swimming?"

Gumball grinned. "I'm up for it. I have an intense interest in hydrology, and I'd love to check out the island's water lens up close."

"Ooo!" Cake said. "Water-polo volley ball? Me and Lord Monochromicorn against the rest of you. And girl, I have to say, I'm impressed. You've totally gotten over your ocean phobia."

Fionna smiled. "I didn't have much of a choice, did I?" she said. "Besides, there's only so many times you can almost die in something before it just doesn't scare you anymore."

GET MORE EPIC
with Epic Tales from
Adventure Time:
The Untamed Scoundrel!

Epic Tales from

ADVENTURE TIME

THE UNTAMED SCOUNDREL

by T. T. MacDangereuse

CHAPTER 1

Lady Gooddog sat glaring at her only son across the breakfast table. "What did you do to Lumpy Space Princess on your picnic yesterday?" she demanded, her voice echoing off the tall ceiling of the dining hall.

"Nothing," Sir Jacobus said with a shrug of his broad shoulders, his muscles rippling under his luxurious golden fur.

"You had to have done something," Lord Gooddog insisted as he helped himself to another large slice of apple breakfast pie.

"I didn't. I swear," Sir Jacobus said, sounding a little defensive. "All I did was eat the sandwiches she made, and then drink the apple juice she'd squeezed, and then take a nap on the blanket that she quilted to celebrate the picnic. After that, Finn and I went to check out the barrel races, which were totally rad." Mr. Finnish Biped, aka Finn, was Sir Jacobus's Hu-manservant. He was known throughout the Kingdom of Plaid for his love of battle and his great loyalty to his lordship, and best friend, Sir Jacobus.

Lady Gooddog shook her head, her eyes raised toward the ceiling. "I can't believe how insensitive you are."

Her son was confused. "It was just a picnic. What's the big deal?"

"The big deal," thundered Lord Gooddog, "is that Lumpy Space Princess was expecting you to propose."

"Propose?" Sir Jacobus sputtered. He had been taking a large swig of apple cider, and his father's comment caught him by such surprise that a bit of the juice sprayed out his nose. "But she's all lumpy," he managed to say after he'd stopped coughing.

"And space princessy," Finn added from where he lounged in a chair, using a toothpick to pry a piece of apple skin out from between his teeth.

Lady Gooddog fixed the servant with an angry glare. "Mr. Biped, do you really think it's appropriate for a servant to sit at the breakfast table with his master's family? Is that what servants do?"

"I don't know," was Finn's reply. "It's what I do and I'm a servant, so yeah, I guess it kind of is."

The lady gave a resigned sigh. "Could you at least take your feet off the table?" she asked.

"Yeah, Finn," Sir Jacobus told him. "That's really gross and some of us are still trying to eat."

"Fine," his manservant said, thumping his feet onto the floor. He reached across the table to help himself to another apple.

Turning back to her son, Lady Gooddog continued with, "Did you ever stop to think why Lumpy Space

Princess went to all that trouble for your picnic?"

"Not really," Sir Jacobus admitted as he finished his apple porridge. "I just figured she likes to do that kind of stuff."

"I don't think you realize how upset the princess really is," his father told him. "She's been on a shopping tirade since yesterday afternoon. All the shop clerks throughout the kingdom have been terrorized." He cocked an ear toward the window. "Listen, I think I can still hear her now."

Everyone was quiet for a moment. It wasn't too difficult to hear the voice of Lumpy Space Princess echoing across the land. "You call that pink?" she roared. "That's, like, totally mauve at best. How dare you try to tell me that mauve is pink! Do you know who I am?"

Then there was another voice, a frightened male voice. It was obvious that he was doing everything within his power to be conciliatory. "I am so sorry,

Miss Lumpy Space. It must be the lighting in here. I sincerely thought it was pink. Let me go and fetch you a pink one from the back."

"That's Lumpy Space Princess to you! I am royalty!" she informed him. There was a loud bang and the sound of glass shattering.

"Oh. Is that what that is?" Sir Jacobus said, scratching his head. "I heard that when I got up this morning, but I thought the kingdom was just infested with dragons again."

"Oh, too bad," Finn said, looking a little disappointed. "I love fighting dragons. That would have been totally math."

Lumpy Space Princess wasn't finished yet. Her tirade continued. They could hear her yelling, "No, I don't want a different size. It's not my job to fit into your stupid clothes. It's your job to design fashion around me."

Sir Jacobus gave his father a penetrating look.

"Are you sure that's not dragons?"

"Yes, I'm sure," Lord Gooddog said, getting a bit hot under his frilled collar. "Listen, Jacobus. This has got to stop. You've broken the heart of almost every maiden in all of Plaid. People are starting to talk. When are you going to choose a wife?"

"A wife?" Sir Jacobus said, a little shocked. "Why would I want a wife? I'm a scoundrel."

"An untamed scoundrel," Finn added, putting his feet back up on the table as he happily munched on the apple.

"It's true," the only child of Lord and Lady Gooddog said with a prideful grin. "No one can tame me."

"Well, you listen here, Mr. Untamed Scoundrel," Lady Gooddog said, getting to her feet and slapping Finn's shoes off the table. "At tomorrow night's ball, you are going to choose a bride. Do you hear me? Because if you don't, you are going to be a very poor untamed scoundrel." Her son was about to protest, but she cut him off. "Either you choose a bride at the ball, or your father and I will disown you and cut you off without a cent."

"Aw, man," Sir Jacobus said. "You guys wouldn't do that, would you?"

"We've already put the wheels in motion," Lord Gooddog said, getting to his feet to stand at his wife's side. They faced their son as a united front. "We sent out an announcement first thing this morning, telling all eligible female guests that it is your intent to choose a bride at the ball."

"What the zip? This really stinks," Sir Jacobus said, crossing his arms over his broad chest. "How the heck am I supposed to do that?"

"I don't know," his mother told him, "but you'd better figure something out by tomorrow evening."

"This really ducks," Sir Jacobus grumbled as he slouched out of the dining hall with his Finn at his side. "What's the point of being an untamed scoundrel if I'm married?"

"Yeah, dude," Finn agreed. "You'd be, like, totally tamed."

"Maybe I should just tell my parents that they can keep their old fortune," Sir Jacobus said, sounding a little sulky. "I mean, I don't really care about the money as long as I can keep living in the castle and have nice clothes and fine food and plenty of servants to do all my stuff for me."

"Yeah," Finn said, pursing his lips a little, "I'm pretty sure they mean you're not going to be able to have any of that stuff, either."

"Doggone it!" Sir Jacobus said with a huff. "Well, I don't think I'd like being poor, so I guess I have to let somebody tame me." He let his broad shoulders sag. "But how am I supposed to choose a bride by tomorrow night?"

"I know!" Finn said, brightening. "I have a plan

that is totally amazing. It will make sure you get the coolest and most awesomest bride ever."

"What?" the Gooddog asked, looking up eagerly. He knew his Hu-manservant and best friend wouldn't let him down.

"We'll hold a tournament. And the girls can compete. With, like, jousting and stuff. And whoever wins the tournament will obviously be supercool, so that's how you'll know who to marry," Finn explained.

"That's a great idea!" Sir Jacobus agreed. "I mean, not the jousting because Mom doesn't like it when I bring horses in the castle. The last time we tried that she totally yelled. But we should definitely have a tournament."

"Okay, cool," Finn said with a smile. "I'll put out an official proclamation letting the ladies know they should come to the ball ready to rumble."

About the Author

The elusive T. T. MacDangereuse is one of the most popular authors in all of Ooo. Although little is known about her private life, it is rumored that she learned the art of storyship at a very young age after being rescued from a pack of jitter-bugging party bears by The Prince of the Pencil Kingdom. She claims that all her story ideas are inspired hallucinations caused by eating too many apple pies.